W9-BBI-172

"Suppose you really did have a fantasy . . ."

Nikki lifted her head and met Nile Bannerman's wary eyes. "But I did," she said. Somehow the fantasy was all tangled up now as she faced the man known to the inner circle of the international bridge playing world as the King of Diamonds.

"Then I have something to make up to you," he told her. "You wanted to kiss a Frenchman, but I'm only half French." The warm hush of his voice was curiously at odds with the intensity of his words. "You should demand twice as much."

He took her mouth with a confident sureness that caused the trembling within her to resonate like a drumbeat along her spine. Oh yes, in Paris had been the promise it could be like this.

He shifted his mouth to trace her upper lip until she blindly sought his kiss once more. But his mouth lingered exquisite centimeters above hers as he said, "Who are you *really*, Nikki Damon?"

Melissa Forsythe says that she likes to write about the redemptive power of life and provide heartwarming entertainment in the process. She also likes to set her books in the glamorous foreign locations she's had the pleasure to spend time in on her travels. The author is happily married and when she isn't traveling, often to compete in tournament bridge competition, she and her family live in Alabama.

Books by Melissa Forsythe

HARLEQUIN ROMANCE
2750—THE PERFECT CHOICE

Don't miss any of our special offers. Write to us at the following address for information on our newest releases.

Harlequin Reader Service
901 Fuhrmann Blvd., P.O. Box 1397, Buffalo, NY 14240
Canadian address: P.O. Box 603,
Fort Erie, Ont. L2A 5X3

Queen of
Hearts

Melissa Forsythe

Harlequin Books

TORONTO • NEW YORK • LONDON
AMSTERDAM • PARIS • SYDNEY • HAMBURG
STOCKHOLM • ATHENS • TOKYO • MILAN

ISBN 0-373-03035-5

Harlequin Romance first edition February 1990

PROLOGUE

IT WAS BEAUTIFUL beyond description, scarlet, orange and gold, blazing like the living fire from which it took its name: fire opal.

Nile Bannerman cradled it in his palm, knowing that if he dropped it, the fragile opal would shatter into a hundred sparks, like a log exploding in a campfire. A little larger than a robin's egg, the jewel was not a perfect oval. One end tapered to a rounded point while the other swelled, dimpling into a double curve.

"What did I tell you Nile?" Gruff and jovial, the voice drew a courtesy glance from Bannerman's deep blue eyes before they fastened once more on the opal. "Was it worth a detour to see this before you go home to Paris?"

Bannerman wasn't sure. Red as the Australian earth from which it came, the jewel was born of the infernal heat of the opal mines, fire in the palm of his hand.

Fragile. Nile Bannerman didn't deal in the fragile, only in the eternal and the indestructible.

"I'm a diamond man," he said, but his statement was incomplete, not a final refusal.

"Take it for your sister, then. See what she can make of it." The other man spoke with the confidence of one who knew the worth of his offering. "It's not the largest opal in the world, but there's not a flaw in it. It's absolutely perfect.''

This Bannerman didn't dispute. "What about the shape?" he asked. "So irregular."

The gruff old voice chortled. "You're holding it wrong." Deft fingers gave the opal a quarter turn. What Nile saw then nearly took his breath away. Quite unnecessarily the old fellow said, "It's heart shaped. At the slightest movement it seems to beat like it was alive."

Bannerman took the opal, and when he returned to Paris he brought it into his sister's workshop-boutique near the House of Bannerman. "See what you can do with this, Elaine." Gingerly his fingers unfolded the white paper that was wrapped around the stone.

"Oh—" Silence followed Elaine's soft utterance. Then she spoke, more to herself than to Nile. "The heart on fire."

"Hold it," Nile told her, and he watched as the flaming opal took on new life from the slightest movement of his sister's hand.

Elaine was mesmerized. "I know exactly what it should be, Nile."

"Fine." His answer was so crisp Elaine looked up in surprise. "I'm no judge of opals, and I don't want to be. They crack and shatter." They broke, like hearts. "Diamonds last forever."

"Opals last, too, if they're cared for," said Elaine. Some things were taboo to speak of, and she was dangerously near one of them. "Wouldn't you care for this if it were given to you?"

Anyone but Elaine would have missed the slight narrowing of Nile's eyes, and the microscopic twist betraying tension at the corner of his mouth. She'd struck a nerve. Good. It was time someone did. He'd kept himself so long in a prison he didn't even recognize the bars. If the sight of that breathtaking heart disturbed him, it must be a good sign.

"That's something I don't have to worry about," said Nile. "It's in your hands, for now. You take care of it."

To his retreating back she said, "I will."

Once in the weeks that passed Nile mentioned the stone, and Elaine merely said, "I'm working on it."

"I thought you knew exactly what to do with it."

"What to do with it, yes, but how to do it—that had to be perfect."

"Why don't you wait for a commission?" Nile asked. "Your best work comes from inspiration, when you know who you're designing for."

"I have someone special in mind," said Elaine.

It took time to design the setting and even longer to execute it, but finally Elaine was satisfied. Then she waited for one of Nile's visits to the shop.

"Wait up front where the light is good. I have something to show you," she called to him. Elaine carried a black velvet form to the counter where Nile stood, making a ceremony of placing the form and turning it around.

Fire blazed. The setting was so simple Nile didn't even notice the gold. The opal hung slightly tilted, at exactly the angle of a beating heart. Even lying against the black velvet the message in the flame was powerful. At a woman's breast . . .

Nile's reaction wasn't what Elaine expected. "An anatomy lesson? What was so difficult it took you months to do the work?" His response was forced.

Elaine could tell that her brother was moved, more than he wanted her to see.

Elaine smiled. "Turn it over. The work is on the back."

Alone it would have been an ornament of surpassing beauty. Elaine had fashioned gold into an intricate design and wreathed the jewel with a hidden message. "My heart is in your keeping."

"It's meant to be a gift to a bride," Elaine explained. "A perfect gift for perfect love."

Twice a clock ticked before Nile resumed breathing. He slowly returned the pendant to rest on its velvet form, his eyes lingering on the opal, as if trying to deny its very existence.

The shop door opened, the jangling bells on the handle snapping Nile's attention back. An odd-looking couple entered, he darkly handsome in a sharp-featured way and tanned mahogany, she regal in her furs and confident of her perfect beauty, cool and distant.

The man's smile was almost greedy when he spied the opal.

"Would a fire like that melt your ice?" he asked the woman.

Her mouth hinted at a smile. "I don't know," she answered. "Buy it for me and we'll see."

The man asked, "You are Miss Elaine?" He made an astonishing offer, twice what Elaine would have asked for the opal.

Elaine replied, "This is from Mr. Bannerman's private collection. It isn't mine to sell."

The man's hooded eyes became slits. The woman's mouth assumed a pout. Looking at Nile with provocation and an open invitation in her eyes, she purred, "I want it."

"It's not for sale," Nile answered, his voice harsher than he realized.

If the other man saw or cared about that blatant display, he didn't show it. Dismissing Elaine, he turned a calculating smile on Nile and named another figure.

Nile refused.

"Are you going to let him do this to you?" the woman taunted. Things were taking an ugly turn.

"Patience, patience," the man crooned. "You know you always get what you want."

The crooning changed to a spitting sound when he spoke to Nile and Elaine. "Mr. Bannerman. Miss Bannerman." The man appeared to be filing away information. With one finger he gave the opal pendant an insolent tweak. "She likes this," he said. "She will have it. It is only a matter of finding what I have to do to convince you."

The bells on the closing door clanged as the couple left. Elaine took a soft cloth to wipe away the traces of the man's touch, then gently laid the opal to rest against the velvet form.

"That's what the world is really like," Nile said bitterly. "That man's in thrall to a conniving witch, and I'll bet she's as faithless as every other woman in the world. So much for your 'bridal gift.' It was a beautiful idea, Elaine, but you didn't put a blessing on that heart—it was a curse. No man should be fool enough to give his whole heart—there's not a woman on earth fit to receive it."

"You don't believe that, Nile, or you'd have sold the opal," Elaine replied.

"*You* don't believe it," Nile countered. He pointed at the pendant, saying, "That's *your* act of faith, not mine. Show me someone who can love like that, Elaine, and I'll *give* him the opal. He deserves it. Until then—" Nile took the pendant from the form and put it in a jewel case "—it can join the rest of my useless private collection at House of Bannerman. I'm going to lock this heart in the vault. I doubt it will ever see the light of day."

CHAPTER ONE

NIKKI DAMON walked with a spring in her step, despite the miles she'd already covered. "It's been a glorious morning," she said, her voice ringing with pleasure. "And it's going to be a heavenly afternoon. Four days ago I thought I had terminal jet lag, but that's all over now."

"Just in time to develop a terminal case of 'tourist feet'? Have a little mercy!"

Nikki sent a sparkling smile to the woman who walked beside her. "My feet haven't touched the ground since we got to Paris. Oh, Sybil, thank you for these extra days."

"Purely business," said Sybil Considine. "And just plain common sense. We couldn't start the duplicate bridge tournament still running on California time. This stopover is killing two birds with one stone."

Sybil's firm was doing just enough business to keep the time in Paris from being an outright gift, but Nikki would never see it any other way.

Sybil prompted her again. "Your feet might not touch the ground, but mine are definitely making contact. Furthermore, I'm starving."

It had been a long time since their breakfast of coffee and croissants. Nikki was running on pure excitement, but Sybil's need for fuel was a more basic kind.

"Do you realize where we are?" Nikki asked.

"Outside the Grand Palais," Sybil replied.

"Ah, more than that, Sybil. More." Nikki stood open-armed, presenting and embracing the view of a broad avenue, all at the same time. "Just up there is the Champs Élysées."

"Aha...your list." Sybil cocked her head knowingly. "Does this mean I have to walk another mile?"

"We won't walk," Nikki responded. "We'll stroll. We'll saunter."

"You do it with your feet, don't you?"

"Come on Syb," Nikki urged, laughing. "Strolling takes no energy at all. Besides, a sidewalk café isn't a sidewalk café unless it's on the Champs Élysées."

Stroll they did, slowly passing under the deep green of broad-leafed chestnut trees. Nikki had arrived to find Paris chilled and gray under a fine misting rain that encouraged her to stay in and rest and let her mind and body catch up with the time difference between Paris and the California coast. Soon she was sight-seeing with a vengeance, braving the chilly spring rains to traipse through the museums and art galleries. She soaked it up, everything from antiquity to modern times, but she'd been far too long indoors. Let it rain. What she wanted now was the boulevards of Paris.

This day was different from the moment it began. The misting rain cleared away, and a gentle sun warmed the clean-washed air. Nikki and Sybil declared an outdoor holiday for themselves, beginning with a walk through the narrow winding streets of Montmartre. Around every corner there was something to charm and captivate.

Nikki carried with her something Sybil referred to in ponderously solemn tones. The list. It was compiled partly from guidebooks, partly from Sybil's travel experience and in part from every movie Nikki had ever seen. "I want to do everything," Nikki had said. "I want to taste the wine and break the bread and..." See the Hotel de Ville by lamplight, browse the bookstalls by the river, breathe the springtime air of France. Nikki gestured, helplessly unable to describe it all. "Oh, everything!"

Sybil had promised that she would and had insisted Nikki write "everything" down.

Green benches lined the pathway where they walked, and from the blossoming chestnut trees, petals fell like pastel rain. They floated softly down upon a couple seated there, oblivious to Nikki's passing, oblivious to the traffic, lost to everything but each other.

"That's Paris," Nikki said with a wistful sigh. "How can I ever pay you back for this?"

"I've heard enough thanks from you," Sybil argued. "You long ago paid back in spades everything you think I've given. I take that back," she corrected hastily, "you do owe me. Food you promised. Food you will deliver. Now!"

They found a café with small round tables crowded onto the very busy sidewalks. The chairs were a jumble, and people had to detour around them.

"Should we go on?" Nikki asked.

"Wait a minute," Sybil said. Then, "Just look at you. There are chestnut petals all over you. There are even some in your hair."

Nikki brushed at her sleeve, but the petals clung to the loosely knitted sweater. She plucked them away, letting them drop to the pavement. Someone in the crowd jostled her against a table, and Nikki started to

apologize, but the man who sat there was hidden behind an open newspaper, and he didn't budge. All he
did was shift a pair of long legs out of the way and go
on reading.

Once or twice a man in passing would turn inquisi-
tive eyes her way, taking in the heathery sweater and
the narrow pants that hugged the lines of her legs,
more concealing than revealing. Nikki chuckled softly
at the patented Gallic gleam, thinking it was for her
burden of flowers, and not for the way she moved. She
had that appealing look of a girl just past adoles-
cence, when coltish awkwardness first turns into long-
limbed grace. She didn't look long enough to see how
some turned back for one more glance at her.

Nikki reached up to find the petals in her hair,
caught in the thick and lustrous wine-dark braid. The
petals were so soft she held one or two for a moment,
pale and delicate, against the fair peach of her cheek.
Another gift, she thought to herself, a garland from
the heart of Paris. A secret smile curved her mouth.

"Here's a table," Sybil called. "Come on."

Behind Nikki the newspaper rattled and snapped. A
waiter was about to serve the seated customer, and she
was in the way. Nikki moved on.

Nikki had to thread her way through the jumble of
chairs, and she realized why the waiters had to be so
supple. She couldn't walk. She could only dance her
way to the table where Sybil sat.

"Whew! I thought all that gliding around was just
for effect," Nikki said. "Have you mastered the side-
walk-café slither?"

"I have mastered Potage St. Germaine," Sybil replied as steaming bowls of soup appeared. "At least

the waiters know a desperate woman when they see one."

Being late had its advantages. The hectic pace in the café was slowing down. The tables were full, but the diners were having a leisurely cup of coffee, whiling away the time in conversation. Nikki listened to the flow of French voices, though the words went by so fast she could hardly comprehend them. Instead of struggling to understand, she simply let the language make beautiful sounds—far more interesting than actually knowing what the stock market was doing, or where to get one's car serviced.

"Oh, this is delicious."

"I take back everything I've said," Sybil announced. "It's a good thing we're doing so much walking."

Nikki agreed. "It burns off our sins *de cuisine* before they come to rest on our derrieres."

A waiter freshened the coffee as Sybil asked for another look at the list. "You're really making headway." Sybil's eyes scanned the list once more. "What's this you've scribbled down here at the bottom? 'April in Paris'? Too late, Nikki. It's May."

"Oh, that," Nikki said offhandedly. "It's a code."

"For what?"

"It was a—it's just a—I guess you might say it's a fantasy." Nikki hadn't really meant to write it on her list, but when Sybil had suggested she write down everything she wanted to do, Nikki'd given in to dreams. There were other things besides monuments and paintings and the panorama of history. Paris meant something more, and with a lift in her heart Nikki had hastily added one more thing. "April in Paris."

"Why Nicole! I do believe you have a romantic streak."

"A mile wide," Nikki confessed. "I just don't have much time to indulge it."

Sybil gave a wry chuckle of sympathy. "Sometimes I think I've pushed you too hard, robbed you of a private life," she said.

Nikki's lips curled into a smile. "You pushed me all the way to Paris, Syb. That's not robbery."

"It will be robbery if you don't tell me about April in Paris."

Nikki hesitated, then plunged in. Sybil might as well know how wide that romantic streak really was. "This is the world capital of romance. Love with a capital *L*. Imagine every movie you've ever seen about Paris. In my favorite dream I'm walking along the Seine while music is playing. It's spring and there are stalls filled with flowers. Then I turn and see a handsome Frenchman and run into his arms, and he whirls me around and kisses me while all of Paris looks on smiling."

Nikki grinned sheepishly, having admitted there was something outrageous she wanted. No, not really wanted...only played with in a fantasy. In real life no one whirled around amid the flowers and the music. She cleared her throat and said, "We can walk from here to the Arc de Triomphe and take the Metro home. It isn't far."

"In a minute." Sybil sipped her coffee. Her eyes sparkled with mischief. "Would it have to be at the flower market?"

"What?" Nikki asked.

"Your kiss. Does it have to be at the flower market along the Seine?"

Laughing, Nikki replied, "No, silly, anywhere in Paris would do. What's a mile or so to a fantasy?"

"Well, Nikki, you don't have time to wait around for your Frenchman to appear. You'll just have to do it yourself. You have Paris. You even have chestnut blossoms. Why not find your Frenchman?"

"Sybil!"

"Why not? It's on your list, Nikki, and you swore an oath you'd do every single thing on it."

"I don't believe you!" Nikki exclaimed. "At your age, in your position . . . you ought to know better."

"At your age," Sybil said pointedly, "in your position you ought to let loose and do it. I think it's a great idea. You'll have a kiss in Paris to remember all your life. Then you can walk off into the sunset and leave your Frenchman smiling an enigmatic smile."

Nikki could only gape at Sybil, calm, collected and utterly serious. She began to laugh.

"If you were going to do it, who would you pick? How about that man over there?" Sybil gestured discreetly.

"Not my type," said Nikki, playing along. "Looks too suave. We want an enigmatic smile, remember? Not a Gallic shrug." Quickly she dismissed another candidate, obviously married. Then Sybil's eyebrow rose a fraction.

"Look over your shoulder, Nikki, behind you. What about him?"

The man sat alone, reading a newspaper. Could he be the one whose table Nikki had bumped? His left hand idly stretched out, and lean, bronzed fingers surrounded a china cup. Nikki's eyes hesitated briefly, and she gave a little smile as she noticed those fingers, curling around the rim of the cup, were bare.

She was not a good judge of height, but he appeared to be tall. He'd made an angular adjustment of his long legs to stretch them beneath his table. Nikki let her glance linger for a moment, and she wondered with just a touch of admiration how he'd managed it.

He was the same man who'd been sitting there. She recognized the cordovan loafers on his feet. Odd, she thought, how a simple thing like shoes could speak volumes about the man. Good leather and well cared for, she registered in a twinkling, comfortable and yet obviously expensive. The gray slacks he wore draped well along the length of muscular legs.

Not wanting to be caught openly admiring the man's physique, Nikki quickly darted a glance at his face.

He was intent upon his paper, a scowl touching his brow as he read, so Nikki continued to study him. Beneath a jacket of mixed gray tweed he wore a dark turtleneck sweater. That look of casual restraint was sharply in contrast with something decidedly rakish in his appearance.

The line of his jaw was strong and tensed—the news he was reading made him angry. No, Nikki decided, there was urgency and purpose in the way his brows arched. She was certain if she could see them clearly his eyes would flash a steely glint.

His hair was very dark, cut not quite short enough to discipline the crisp curl that, grown longer, would have made him look a little like a pirate. He didn't exactly fit Nikki's idea of typical Gallic good looks. He was a bit too rugged; the strength of his features hadn't quite given in to the polish of sophisticated charm. He made sophisticated charm look tame.

A movement rippled the wide shoulders of his jacket, a coiled tension belying the easy motion of his arm as he replaced his coffee cup. The pirate didn't look like a man who would be content to smile a mysterious smile. Yet there was something about him that fit her image. If flowers bloomed and music played, it would be for someone like him.

The shadowy figure out of fantasy now had substance, form and face, and he was overwhelmingly attractive.

"Well?" The voice at Nikki's elbow jolted her back to reality. "I'll never tell."

Nikki made an effort to suppress the smile playing at the corners of her mouth, but the twinkle in her dark brown eyes gave her away. "Made to order," she replied.

"What are you waiting for? It's spring. This is Paris. You'll be in Nice on Sunday. Nikki, seize the day. Do it."

Nikki wanted to protest that she couldn't, that it was only a fantasy better left where it belonged, in dreaming. But the man was making ready to leave, reaching into his pocket for a few francs to leave on the table. Without a word Sybil gathered Nikki's purse up with her own and secured her franc notes underneath a saucer. In a sudden gesture she reached for Nikki's list before starting up the boulevard. The faint stir of her passing fanned cool air against Nikki's cheek, warm where a blush was stealing.

Nikki rose as the man rose, making her way past the small crowded tables. She almost turned aside when his glance caught hers, the merest pause, too swift for him to take in more than a lithe form moving with uncommon grace.

He reached the open sidewalk and turned to face her, now openly admiring what he saw. On feet that seemed not her own, Nikki walked toward him. She was close enough to see the color of his eyes, a deep and brilliant blue. They widened in surprise as Nikki walked straight to him.

Her voice was breathless, almost husky. She'd come this far, she couldn't turn back now. Her guidebook French would have to serve. She selected her words with care, to say, "Pardon me, I would like a moment of your time." Before the man could reply, Nikki moved nearer, and as he realized what she intended, his eyes flashed and narrowed, but he didn't move away.

He was taller than she, and when her hand circled behind his neck, he bent toward her. Nikki's fingers brushed against the smooth folds of his sweater and came to tangle in the thick soft curls of his hair. She meant to touch his lips only briefly with her own, not to feel his arms tighten around her, pulling her fast against the hardness of his chest. She never meant that first, almost fleeting touch to be followed by the slow, firm and deepening pressure of a kiss that was neither his nor hers.

Her lips warmed to the breath of his muffled exclamation and fired at the touch of his mouth. Crushed against him, Nikki breathed the air of Paris spring clinging to his clothing and a subtle trace of clean fresh fragrance on his skin. Her fingertips tingled with a rushing sensitivity as they strayed from his hair to move in stealthy intimacy along the back of his neck and encounter a greater warmth where the collar of his sweater rose.

Nikki was acutely aware of the outline of her body held firmly pressed against his, embraced, and of his lips moving across hers, not yet ready to break away. Then blue, luminous, world-filling color held her too entranced to realize that his gaze was sweeping over her. She was spellbound in a moment truer and more real than the imagined swirl of flowers or the music of a dream. Spellbound...until she saw her own eyes reflected in his.

Suddenly the boulevard traffic noises blared in her ears, a jarring intrusion into the soundless moment in his arms. Nikki stepped back, eyes startle-wide, and she was nearly trembling with apprehension. The man released his hold on her.

His face was coming into focus. How could she look at him? How could she dare to look away? Nikki took one step backward.

He was stock-still, but he seemed to be looming taller, his shoulders tensing so that they looked wider than before. Nikki felt the rush of her heated breath escaping through parted lips. She retreated another step.

In the dark brilliance of his eyes a new spark flashed. His mouth curved menacingly, and he cursed.

Nikki turned and fled.

She looked back. He stood rooted to the sidewalk, as if he'd been struck by thunder, his fingers raking through his dark unruly curls.

A few stumbling steps, and Nikki looked back again. He was still there. Then he retreated a few steps and picked up his newspaper. He rolled it into a cylinder and beat it against the palm of his hand. Once, twice.

This time Nikki ran. The storm of thoughts clamoring in her head kept up a wild tempo to match the frantic sound of her footsteps on the pavement. Her heart pounded against her ribcage. When she took one more furtive look down the boulevard, the man was gone.

Sybil was in sight, just ahead. With an effort Nikki fell into pace alongside her.

"Temporary insanity," she said, panting. "That's what I'll plead if he comes after me." She walked faster, but her footsteps couldn't outrun the turmoil of her feelings, and she wondered—much too late—if she had embarrassed that Frenchman, who certainly didn't smile an enigmatic smile.

NIKKI SILENTLY growled a warning to herself every time she thought of him. *Him.* The man without a name. The man whose face haunted her even now and made her wish the fantasy were real. With more time to think of it she'd have been shuddering with guilt, but the days were so few and so full there was little time left for self recrimination. She was determined to keep her mind on the purpose of this trip. Most of all she couldn't let Sybil down.

Nikki Damon had long since stopped reflecting on the curious turn of events that had brought her here. When her life took her into uncharted territory, she was eager for the journey. Nikki was firm in her belief that she was a simple person. It was only her life that was complex. As long as she held on to the traditions that nourished her roots, as long as she remembered how deep those roots were, she never foundered. Then she could try anything.

Her father ran a small business, and it was successful enough to provide for his family. Her mother kept a comfortable home. Nikki was accustomed to the way her mother treated her homemaking role as "helping out" instead of the vitally necessary job it was. But Nikki saw, and thought about it, and when she tried her wings, it was to make a place for herself that wouldn't be just "helping out."

Opportunity, when it came, was far away, and it was the biggest step she'd ever taken.

"California?" her father had said. "If you want to go away, move to Atlanta. At least we'd see you now and then."

"We could get there if you needed us." Mothers always said that. Nikki had seen the gleam of encouragement in her mother's eyes, and it spoke louder than the automatic maternal plea.

She went to work for Stanhope and Considine, and it was the beginning of a four-year roller coaster ride. Nikki made a reputation for herself, earned a promotion to project manager and finally a move onto the corporate floor as assistant to the president, Sybil Considine.

"Nikki-Nerves-of-Steel" was what Sybil called her. If Sybil Considine told her to do a job, she did it. *Impossible* wasn't in her vocabulary. Her former boss had bragged once too often that he gave the impossible jobs to Nikki because she always got them done. Mrs. Considine had checked her out and promptly stolen Nikki for her assistant.

Shortly afterward Nikki had been playing a lunchtime game of bridge when her new boss dropped by to watch. California-blond and tan, still beautiful at nearly fifty, Sybil Considine was a high-ranked bridge competitor with a world championship to her credit.

Nikki was in awe of her.

Sybil slipped into a chair beside Nikki and watched her play a hand. The contract was shaky and difficult to play, and Nikki hadn't time to be nervous, even if this was an international champion looking over her shoulder.

"Tell me why you played the hand that way," Sybil said. When she'd heard Nikki's explanation, her face broke into a delighted smile. "That's a very advanced play you made. Did it bother you having me watch?"

"Not really," Nikki replied. "It bothered me more that I had to make the contract."

"I was right in my estimation of you," Sybil said. "You are not an ordinary girl, Nikki-Nerves-of-Steel." An evening or two playing bridge with Sybil brought Nikki the surprise of her life.

"This will be hard work and sacrifice. You'll study like you've never studied before, and I'll have you in tournament competition before you think you're ready. But I'm a born mentor and a good teacher, and you have a flair for the game. Nikki Damon, we're going to make a champion out of you."

Nikki had more than a flair—she had a passion for the game, for the competition that dealt her first the bitter humiliation of defeat and then the sweet taste of victory. In two years Nikki was taking the West Coast by storm. Sybil did drive her hard, but Nikki loved it. It wasn't sacrifice.

Her first doubts came when Sybil insisted she was ready for world-class competition. A new championship, each team commercially sponsored, would be played on the Riviera. Sybil was determined to field a team, and Nikki would be on it.

"Syb, I've never even played east of the Rockies, and you're talking about Europe. They'll eat me alive."

"We've beaten world champion pairs. We won't have to hang our heads in Nice."

Nikki was uncertain, even in the face of Sybil's optimism, but *impossible* still wasn't in her vocabulary. If Sybil could find four other players who'd take a chance on her, she would give it all she had.

Then the roller coaster became an airliner to carry her to Paris for a week of sight-seeing and preparation before the competition began.

Thank heaven she had so little time left in Paris. Every time she went out it was the same. In every crowd there was a tall dark head, and every glimpse startled her, sending eager little thrills of excitement down her spine, soon to turn into twinges of dread. What if . . . ?

It was clear to Nikki she'd never know a moment's peace until she was safely in Nice.

NO SOONER had Nikki checked into the chateau-styled hotel facing the Mediterranean than she dumped her luggage and headed for the beach. She was in and out of her hotel room too fast to take in the luxury of it, so fast indeed that she had to go back for a pair of sandals to protect her feet from the shingle beach.

Nikki left her hat and wrap on a rented mattress and waded into the brilliant blue sea. The beach was crowded with gleaming sun-bronzed bodies, and the air was fragrant with coconut tanning oils. Few braved the chilly waters, preferring to laze in the afternoon sun.

Nikki returned from her dip in the sea, stretched out on the mat with her hat over her face and let her mind simply drift. Warmed on one side, she turned onto her stomach, idly surveying the scene.

The bikini that had seemed so daring when she bought it was by far the most modest on the beach. Is the law of gravity suspended here? she wondered. Rather than be caught blatantly staring, she cupped her chin in her palm and looked out at the impossible blue of the sea. The color fascinated her. It was as blue as . . . Maybe the beach wasn't such a good idea.

On a lovely sheltered terrace of the hotel, Nikki found a mob of bridge players, and when she spotted a member of another American team, she cheerfully joined the crowd. Here she found unknowns like herself, as well as the luminaries she'd only seen in pictures.

One held a special fascination. Emilio Orsini of Italy was a player so formidable he was legend. Nikki had imagined him ten feet tall and surrounded by a blazing aura of invincibility. Orsini's reputation kept Nikki at a distance. She wouldn't know what to say to a man who'd dominated bridge for twenty years, but she did steal surreptitious glances at him as she took a glass from the refreshment tray.

"Sizing up your next victim?" The deep baritone voice behind her was laden with sarcasm, low and softly menacing. That voice was disturbingly nearby, and yet the question couldn't be meant for her.

The voice continued, "Poor soul doesn't know what a shock he has in store for him."

Nikki's curiosity overcame her sensible judgment, and she turned abruptly to see who was speaking in such a tiger's growl.

Her fingers gripped the icy glass in a spasm of shock. It was *him*. A wicked spark lit his eyes, and his smile was more one of cynical scorn than amusement as he looked into Nikki's panic-stricken eyes.

"You!" she finally said, half choking as she spoke.

"Yes. Very definitely. Me."

He didn't touch her, and yet Nikki felt as if his hands imprisoned her in an iron grip. She didn't dare move.

His eyes held a hot and dangerous light. "I've been watching you stalk your unsuspecting prey, but before you spring on him, young lady, you have some explaining to do."

"I'm not springing..." Nikki protested. Furious crimson colored her cheeks and burned into her temples. Flustered, she blurted out, "I'm not in the habit—"

"I know very well what you're in the habit of doing," he cut her off sharply. "And before you do it again, you'll answer to me."

CHAPTER TWO

"OH, NO! You're not French!" He'd spoken to her in fluent English.

"Well, that explains everything." His well-defined brows quirked from ferocious scowl to ironic arch. "It's all crystal clear to me now."

"No, I..." Nikki's cheeks were burning. "I *will* explain, I want to. You see, I—"

"Nikki!" A bearlike hug surrounded her as a hearty voice sounded over her shoulder, addressing the man whose face now assumed a casual mask. "You won't mind, will you, if I steal Nikki for just a minute."

"Not at all," he said a trifle too smoothly. "Catch you later...Nikki."

The expression in his eyes barely changed, and yet the challenge in them left Nikki feeling as if she would indeed be caught.

Nikki escaped from the terrace as quickly as she dared. Between rounds of introductions she made furtive efforts to find her nemesis, but he had disappeared. She prayed he would stay out of sight until she was safely in her room.

Unpacking gave her a legitimate excuse to linger in her room, pressing clothes, making sure she had all her study notes in order, giving unaccustomed time and attention to her bath and her grooming.

If she could hide here long enough, she wouldn't have to show her face until the party the World Bridge Federation was giving to kick off the tournament.

Nikki rang the Considine suite. "Sybil, SOS! He's *here*!"

"Whoa, slow down, Nikki. Who is here?"

"That man, from Paris. He's here in Nice, in this very hotel, and he's mad as hell. What are we going to do?"

"What do you mean *we*?" Sybil asked between bursts of laughter. "He's all yours, Nikki."

"Sybil!"

For a second the phone was silent. "By the way, Nikki, what *are* you going to do?"

WHEN NIKKI entered the ballroom that night she half expected to find him waiting at the door. Quickly she realized that among three hundred competitors she could lose herself, so she relaxed a bit.

A young pair from the Italian team seemed bent on starting a mild flirtation with Nikki, bringing her puff pastries filled with shallots in cream sauce, and re-plenishing her wineglass with every sip. Nikki found them entertaining, although she couldn't get them to say a serious word about bridge.

There was an extravagantly delicious meal, flaw-lessly served. Nikki felt so secure, so well hidden, that she stopped searching the room for one face among the crowd. When the dinner service was cleared and the orchestra went from subdued music to a stronger rhythm, she was quickly besieged with offers to dance.

Nikki's mood was bright and lively, and she made a striking appearance on the dance floor. The silky swirl of her long black skirt exposed dainty sandals on her feet. Her blouse was scooped at the neck, setting off the triple layers of black chiffon and beaded black embroidery. Her hair was down, full and luxuriant, as it swung freely to her shoulders. With fair sun-kissed skin against the black of the dress and the deep rich sheen of her hair, the effect was elegant.

Nikki was taking a rest after an exuberant dance with one of her teammates. High color played along her cheeks, and the lamplight at the table made her skin glow like cream. The orchestra music slowed into a romantic ballad, but as yet no one left the round table where she sat. The music was soothing.

"Why hello, Nikki." The purring tiger voice just behind her was anything but soothing. Breaking glass couldn't have startled her more.

Automatically her nearest tablemate edged his chair toward his wife, making a space beside Nikki, who looked over her shoulder into the eyes of a buccaneer sizing up his prize. Didn't anyone else see that wicked pirate look, or hear the note of anticipation that teased so mockingly in his voice? He was too strong and too vital a presence to be civilized by the formal black and white of evening wear.

It was madness and she knew it, but Nikki too was making room.

He pulled a chair into the circle and said casually, "Don't bother doing the introductions, Nikki," and turned away before she could reply. "I'm Nile Bannerman," he said, introducing himself around the table with an ease that left her both envious and dismayed.

Nikki shot a look across the table at Sybil, who met her eyes with a mischievous twinkle. "Ah yes, Mrs. Considine," Nile was saying. "I've heard your name, of course." He knew her name apparently, but not her face. He gave no sign of recognition, and Nikki was sure Nile hadn't seen Sybil that day in Paris.

"Now," he said, purring at Nikki like a tiger with a juicy morsel and giving her a look that underscored his intention to concentrate on her, "we have a lot to catch up on . . . shall we do it here?"

He couldn't. He wouldn't! Not here in front of all her friends. "Oh!" Nikki gulped. "Let's dance," she said quickly, and was instantly on her feet.

"Whatever you like." Lucifer could probably put on such an enchanting smile, just before he used his pitchfork.

Nile led Nikki to the edge of the dance floor, and before her sandals touched the parquet surface, he pulled her into his arms. She ought to resist, go like a schoolgirl to the corner for a dressing-down, but how good he felt, how solid. He kept her from stumbling as she swung into his clasp.

There was sweet treachery in the way her body melded with his, following the slow and sensuous music. The pressure of her fingertips against the fabric of his dinner jacket was hesitant, but even that was too much like a caress. When in dismay she pulled her hand away, Nile drew her even closer and tightened his hold.

"Why so shy all of a sudden, Nikki Damon?" Nile asked, and even his murmur was a taunt.

"How do you know my name?" Nikki answered his question with one of her own.

"In cases of intimate contact it's customary to at least learn the lady's name, and if the lady doesn't tell, the gentleman must have ways of finding out." In case the tone of his voice didn't carry his message, he added, "At least those are the rules in my book, and R. N. Bannerman always plays by the rules. You should, too."

Nikki started to tell him she wasn't playing, but there was a tiny sliver of truth in what he said. Dreams weren't games, but how was he to know?

"Isn't it a marvelous coincidence that we should meet again in Nice, with so much to talk about?"

He was pushing her, just a little too far.

"It isn't marvelous, but it is a coincidence," Nikki replied, and she was serious. She leaned back to look at him, her head tilted to meet his eyes. "Look, you don't have to pretend you know me to show good form," she said crisply. "I'll tell you what you want to know, and you can be on your way."

"So you can look up Orsini, and maybe ask him for 'a moment of his time' like you did me? He'd be just as glad to give it to you as I was." Nikki averted her gaze. "That was what you asked for wasn't it, a moment?"

"I didn't mean . . . oh, please, let me explain."

"Not yet, dear Nikki. Explanations can come in due course," said Nile, and Nikki had a sudden impression of him slackening up a fishing line, biding his time, playing her out. "I've waited this long. Another few minutes won't matter." For a man so gruffly insistent on an explanation, he'd certainly changed. There was lazy nonchalance in his voice, and the sound of it definitely matched the look of self-satisfaction on his face. He wasn't bothering to hide it from her that he was enjoying himself immensely, and at her expense. "Right now we're dancing." He spun her swiftly to punctuate his statement. "Besides, you said you'd rather dance than catch up on things."

What a beast he was! He knew very well she preferred dancing only to having him do his "catching up" in front of everyone. He'd tricked her into being the one to insist upon it.

Nile seemed to read her thoughts. He eyed her appraisingly and said, "I'm going to find out exactly who Nikki Damon is and why she does the things she does." He made it sound as if she had something to hide. "First we'll go back and visit with your friends. Then we'll make a quiet exit when I'm absolutely sure it's safe to be alone with you."

"What do you mean by that?" Nikki asked indignantly.

"I know what you're capable of doing in public." Nile arched his brows meaningfully. "Shouldn't I wonder what your private behavior is like?"

"You're toying with me," Nikki challenged, but all the while her cheeks were burning. Nile Bannerman was going to wring the last drop of misery out of her, and then he would see that she got what was coming to her.

"Is that the judgment of an expert on toying?" Nile gave her a cynical smile, but suddenly his arm, encircling her waist, relaxed into a gentler embrace. "Yes, I am toying with you, Nikki. And enjoying it. Every bit as much as I enjoyed . . ." He let his voice trail off, clearly certain she would be aware of his meaning.

Nikki knew. The shape of his shoulder was too well remembered, and the way his thick dark hair curled beneath her hand. He'd enjoyed that wretched kiss, and even more than that, he was relishing his ability to torment her.

Nile obviously intended to go on relishing it for just a little longer.

"Look over there," he purred in her ear. "It's the captain of the Argentines. How about asking him for a moment of his time?" He nudged her ever so slightly.

"Wha—? No!"

"No?" His vocal tone had the same swoop as the arch of his eyebrow. "Is it the milieu that puts you off? Are you strictly an outdoor girl?"

Nile Bannerman had a voice made rich and wickedly resonant with laughter barely contained.

"Don't squirm so, Nikki." Now his tone was mock scolding. "Remember, you're the one who'd rather dance than talk."

"I would rather do anything than have *you* talk."

At this the richness of his laughter rang out.

The song ended, and Nile took Nikki back to the table, where someone let loose a new flood of fright in her by asking Nile, "Which team are you with?"

"France Number One," Nile replied easily. "Or I should say, House of Bannerman."

Nikki caught his glance and saw how his eyes narrowed suddenly. He was definitely watching to see how she took the news. Her worst fears were realized. She wasn't going to be able to make her explanation and walk away into the sunset after all. Nile was a bridge player, a dark cloud to loom on her horizon for weeks to come.

She barely caught the end of a phrase, "...thought Bannerman was a much older man."

"Bannerman Senior is," was the answer. "My father. He only plays in Europe now."

"Of course, I remember," someone said, and Nikki realized Nile's name was not unknown to the veterans on the team, "the King of Diamonds, they used to call him."

Nikki quipped, "I suppose that makes you the Knave."

The smile Nile turned upon her was much too warm. "Our Nikki has the most wonderful sense of humor. Perhaps that's why she was such a delight in Paris."

Then came the question that nearly ripped Nikki's composure to shreds. "How do you know Nikki?"

Nile Bannerman was just the kind of man who'd tell.

"It was in Paris that we met, not long ago," Nile said, casually glancing Nikki's way so that only she could catch the threatening gleam in his eye. The space where he'd draped his arm around her chair fairly crackled with electric energy. Met? Nikki thought frantically. "Yes, we met..." Her heart skipped a beat as he went on. "And Nikki was so *unusual*, I couldn't help but want to get to know her better."

Nikki nearly choked at Nile's choice of terms. Her ears burned as Nile added, "If I hadn't promised Nikki we'd get away, I'd stay and tell you my first impression."

"But you did promise," Nikki said quickly, looking him straight in the eye. Her response came faster than the tremor of fright spreading ice along her spine. Nile gave her another one of those cat's-got-the-canary smiles.

He'd engineered it perfectly. Once again she was forced to spirit him away before he humiliated her entirely.

Nile paused briefly, causing Nikki to bump into him in her eagerness to flee. With evident mirth Sybil came to her rescue. "Go," she said. "If you don't entertain her, we'll have to." Nikki didn't dare refuse. She had no doubt that the slightest hesitation on her part would bring on an even more provocative comment from Nile. He'd made it clear that with just a little prompting he would cheerfully describe their meeting and just what it was about Nikki he found so... unusual.

As if bowing to Sybil's insistence, Nile took Nikki's arm and escorted her from the ballroom. Nikki barely noticed the rotunda with its circle of columns and elaborate carpet. The dome of stained glass that had glowed so brilliantly in the afternoon was dark now, muting the ornate chairs grouped in royal purples, carnation reds and Versailles golds. Nile had a swift nod for the costumed staff members as he took her through a door held open by a porter in blue and scarlet cape.

His destination was the Promenade des Anglais just outside. The boulevard stretched for miles along the bay, divided by islands of flowers and palms. The bikini-clad crowd was gone, but the boulevard was lively with strolling couples. Nikki's evening gown would attract no undue attention.

Between the blare of automobiles on the thoroughfare and the rush of waves washing ashore, their conversation would be difficult to follow. For that much Nikki was grateful.

She was grateful, too, that Nile set a moderate pace. Her nervousness wouldn't show so much. They had no sooner reached the seaside walkway than Nile dropped her arm and whirled to face her. "All right, Nikki, I'm ready. Now explain.'' Military commanders gave orders like that. "What exactly were you hoping to accomplish with your little game?"

Nikki took a deep breath. "Mr. Bannerman, I apologize."

"*Mister* Bannerman?" Nile chided. "Isn't it a little late for that? You've had a moment of my time, remember?" Before Nikki could reply he continued. "I didn't ask for an apology, Nikki. I want an explanation. Besides, the last thing in the world I want to hear is that you're sorry."

His voice contained only an echo of the harshness from the afternoon, but this evening's edge of irony was firmly intact. In any other place, at any other time, though, Nikki would have warmed to the mellow richness behind the cutting edge. Here and now she heard only menace, and she knew she was being taken to task.

Anxiously she began. "I've never done anything like that before, and I never will again," she assured him. "It was that darned list . . ."

"That what?"

"The list. Of everything I wanted to do in Paris. Oh, Nile, everything was so wonderful, just the way I'd imagined Paris would be. But everyone dreams . . . of being the one to stand beside the Seine among the flowers and turning around and see—" Nikki caught her lower lip between her teeth. "Everyone dreams of kissing a handsome Frenchman." The words came tumbling out. "I just wrote it on the list, 'April in Paris,' so that no one but me would know. I never intended to do it—I just dreamed about something like that happening. Sybil knew that, when I told her what it meant. It's not like me at all. It was so out of character, we were laughing about it."

"Nikki, what in the world are you talking about?" Nile showed every sign of thinking she was trying to put him off. "Do you expect me to believe Mrs. Considine helped you cook up this little scheme?"

"She didn't help me cook up anything. Please, Nile, don't think badly of Sybil. Neither of us meant any harm. It just . . . got started." She looked at him and felt helplessly unable to make him understand. "She would say to me, '*If* you were going to do it . . .' and she'd point to one man, but he'd be all wrong, and the next one was too suave, and the next one was probably married. But when she said, 'What about him?' well, there you were."

"So you just did it," Nile said flatly, and he shook his head from side to side in disbelief.

"No," Nikki confessed, and it was the hardest thing of all to tell him. "I watched you for a while first." Nikki slanted her head forward, and her hair swung to shield her face from Nile's scrutiny. "You looked so right." The kind of man Nikki could imagine herself kissing. "If only you'd stayed there, reading your paper, it never would have happened. But you were leaving, and I was leaving..." It sounded so feeble an excuse.

Nile stopped walking, and for a moment Nikki thought he was going to make another withering remark, but he only reversed his direction and started walking, wordlessly, back toward the hotel. The brightly lighted chateau was farther away than Nikki realized, and she dreaded the return walk with him.

He was too quiet. It was as if he'd forgotten about her and was totally absorbed by his thoughts. Finally, before they crossed the boulevard at the approach to the hotel, Nikki said, "I'm truly sorry, Nile. I didn't mean to embarrass anyone."

To her amazement he laughed. The sound was genuine, and it surrounded her like balm. "I was surprised, yes, intrigued even, as you might well imagine. But not embarrassed. When a beautiful woman walks up to you on the street and kisses you like that, it's anything but embarrassing." Then he bent down so that his mouth was only inches from her ear, and he whispered to her in a villainous tone, "Besides, you're lying."

Nikki sputtered her denial, but Nile would have none of it.

"That is some tale you've concocted, Nikki, and you can look so darn wide-eyed you're almost convincing."

Nikki wasn't accustomed to being on the defensive. "I haven't concocted anything," she said, but before she could utter another word Nile held up his hand to stop her.

"No, no, no," he scolded. "Before you spin any more yarns, I'd better make a confession of my own. I saw you, Nikki. You knew perfectly well I was there long before Mrs. Considine conveniently spotted just the right Frenchman to fulfill your dreams. You were standing right there, my peach-and-burgundy beauty, dropping chestnut petals at my feet."

"I was not. Well, I was, but I wasn't dropping them at your feet. They were stuck to me."

An ironic, satisfied grin creased Nile's cheek. "That's a little better," he said. "With proper handling you can be coaxed into telling the truth."

"I am telling the truth," Nikki said emphatically. Her nerves were stretched taut, and she had the strangest looking-glass feeling that Nile seriously thought she was lying.

"Nikki, I believe you're sorry if you embarrassed me. I even believe you're sorry you're in hot water now." Then there were bitter undertones in his voice. "But whatever your real reasons, I don't believe you're sorry it was Nile Bannerman you kissed in Paris."

Nikki turned her face away and tried an evasive answer. "I was thoughtless, and I never should have—"

"Nikki..."

"It was such a—" Nile gripped her arms, not painfully but with a steadying force, putting an end to her evasions. Was it such a crime that she was drawn to him? Nikki studied the tops of his shoes. Her voice dropped to a husky register. "No, I'm not sorry it was you."

Nikki lifted her head and met his wary eyes, and as her feelings played so transparently across her face, gone was the stern taskmaster and the rascal who delighted in taunting her. This was the man Nikki had imagined kissing. Even now she could imagine kissing him again.

One instant, and then his face was as wary as before. "Come on," Nile said.

"Where?"

"Why to lock you in, of course. Or do you have plans to go back to the party? I did like your friends, Nikki. I'll bet we could swap some stories together."

"You wouldn't dare," she said.

"Wouldn't I?"

Yes, Nikki decided, he would. She let him propel her through the hotel lobby and into the elevator. At her floor, he left the elevator with her, and the doors whooshed shut behind them. At her door he took her arm.

Nile said, "You are intriguing." Devils danced in his eyes, and she wondered what mischief he could be up to now. "Suppose you really did have a fantasy..."

"I did," Nikki said softly. Paris in the spring and a handsome Frenchman in the dreamy shadows. Somehow the fantasy was all tangled up now, Paris in the shadows...

"It appears I may have something to make up to you," he told her. "You wanted to kiss a Frenchman, but I'm only half French." The warm hush of his voice was curiously at odds with the intensity vibrating in his every word. "From half a Frenchman you should demand twice as much."

Nikki fit so perfectly in his arms, it seemed as if he hadn't been the one to pull her there. He gave her no time to protest, and Nikki had no will to do it. Instead she flowed toward him as if drawn by a powerful current, and with a breathless sigh she lifted her lips to his.

He took her mouth with a confident sureness, the warmth invading its soft inner recesses and spreading deliciously throughout her body. No, she wasn't sorry... never would be sorry it was him.

The pressure of Nile's fingers against her shoulders sent Nikki's arms rising to embrace him. The scent of his crisp, clean shirtfront and a tangy berry aroma on his skin mingled, and they were intoxicating, shooting straight into her brain.

Her lips trembled beneath his, and the trembling resonated like a drumbeat along her spine. Oh, yes, in Paris had been the promise that it could be like this.

He shifted his mouth away from hers only to trace her upper lip with gentle pressure until she blindly sought his kiss once more.

Then he laced his fingers in her hair and drew them down its silky length and pressed the heat of his palm against her throat, where her pulse beat. Nile's mouth was tender upon hers and fierce beyond the tenderness.

At last he drew away. "I never had much use for fantasies," he told her. "I much prefer the real thing." His arms crushed her to him, and his mouth lingered exquisite centimeters above hers, and he said, "Who are you, really, Nikki Damon?" Then he claimed the kiss that bore her name.

Nikki had gone into his arms longing for that kiss. Who was he, that in spite of everything this stranger's kiss was the sweetest she'd ever known? Her fingers stole into the soft-crisp curls where his hair met his nape, and the low moan that vibrated in his throat was electrifying. She wanted to speak his name again, but his mouth imprisoned hers.

It was Nile who summoned up the will to end that kiss. Something flickered across his face, like a shadow of regret. Though his voice was quiet, it was rough to Nikki's ears when he said, "I shouldn't ask questions when I already know the answer."

What had he asked? Nikki's mind was reeling, and the only word on her lips was "Nile." She searched his face, but he wouldn't meet her eyes.

"I won't ask you to invite me in," he said as he took the key from Nikki's unsteady fingers and unlocked the door. "There's too much stardust in your eyes."

Once inside, Nikki leaned against the door, shaken and bewildered. Like a sleepwalker she went to her dressing table and stood before the mirror. She was wide-eyed at the image it contained. The features were familiar but only vaguely so. The cloud of wine-dark hair surrounding her face took her by surprise. It was wildly disarrayed, testimony to the touch of Nile's hands, and oddly appealing. Her mouth was fuller, having been kissed into a yielding tenderness that sent an apprehensive shiver down her spine.

Nikki slipped into a nightgown and crept beneath the light coverlet, wakeful and trying to bring some order into the chaos in her mind.

Nile Bannerman was the most unpredictable man! In the course of a single day he'd run her through the wildest gamut of emotions. On the terrace his eyes had crackled with blue fire when she'd looked into his face. Had he actually imagined she'd kiss Emilio Orsini? In the ballroom those same eyes had been wicked with mirth as he skillfully taunted her with hints of exposure. In spite of herself she chuckled, remembering his words, "Nikki was so *unusual*..."

That first kiss tonight, she was certain, was meant to teach her that she couldn't kiss and run. But the others?

Beyond that Nikki didn't dare to think. She couldn't explain tonight, not even to herself. Nikki drifted at last into a sleep, where everything her conscious mind would not allow could float in and out in dreams, and her voice would not be kept from asking, "What have I done? What has he done to me?"

CHAPTER THREE

NIKKI HAD GOT UP early to start the day with a no-nonsense swim, and now she had one of the small terrace tables to herself. She hoped no one came to sit with her, because her thoughts still were none too steady.

Morning light sparked rainbows from the crystal and shimmered on the fresh bouquet of flowers. She was glad she'd chosen to breakfast on the terrace instead of bothering to go to her room to change. The dining room couldn't compare to the open air.

Her salt-wet hair was escaping into tendrils of curl, and her skin glowed from that invigorating swim. The physical exertion had been just what she needed. The nippy water ought to clear her mind and get her ready for long hours of mental struggle at the bridge table.

She was scooping a morsel of melon onto her spoon when a lean bronzed hand pulled back the chair across from her.

"May I join you?"

"Oh!"

"You do remember me, don't you?" Nile Bannerman gave her his most rascally smile as he took his seat. "Yes, I see you do." He leaned forward, his size diminishing the dainty wrought-iron table and making him seem much closer than he was. The morning light accentuated his vibrant looks, highlighting his

skin against the Arran knit sweater he wore, sparkling in a drop of moisture that still clung to his hair.
He took a very roguelike tone. "It's gratifying to know
I have such an impact on you. Only yesterday you
turned white as a sheet at the sight of me, and today
you're such a lovely shade of pink. Is that sunburn, or
would last night have something to do with it?"

Nikki found her voice. "It's sunburn," she hissed
at him, trying to make a whisper sound like a bark.

"Are you sure?" How could he look so clear-eyed
and guileless when Nikki knew he was full of guile?
"A blush comes and goes, and Nikki, it's a scientific
fact that sunburn doesn't flicker." Nile leaned forward in his chair. "This is a terribly interesting phe-
nomenon. I'd better get a closer look."

"Don't you come near me," was Nikki's instant
reply.

With a short sharp laugh Nile settled back in his
chair. "Nikki, Nikki," he scolded. "Your timing's off.
You are hours late with that one." The more Nikki
tried to shush him, the more Nile's eyes filled with
pure delight. "I can think of a dozen opportunities
you missed. Let's see, there was one..."

"Nile there are people here!"

"How shocking! Of course you're much too delicate to *talk* about...opportunities in a place like this."

Nikki tried the most withering look she could muster.

Nile laughed at her discomfort and gave a little dis-
missive nod of capitulation. "All right, we'll talk
about something safer. How about the weather?"

To Nikki it seemed too swift a giving-in. Just as he
had on the dance floor, Nile gave every impression of

playing out the fishing line a bit. He wouldn't let her off this easily.

"The weather's fine," said Nikki, agreeing to the topic.

"Do you always get in a morning's work while the slugabeds are lazing around?" Nile asked, looking at her closely. "You're hair's wet—you've had a swim."

"Oh, that," Nikki said. Swimming was a safe enough topic. Much safer than anything else she could think of. "Sybil has a theory that physical work complements mental work. She has us all in training."

"Even the one on your team who looks like an unmade bed?"

Nikki nodded. "Especially him. She personally rousts him out and has him run up and down the roads. This team will have sound minds in sound bodies even if it kills us." She was doing really well, she thought. A conversation about the team wouldn't be full of pitfalls.

The corner of Nile's mouth quirked. "I couldn't agree more." Dancing eyes scanned Nikki's face and strayed lower, taking in what was visible of her legs beneath the glass tabletop. "I've never seen a sounder body than yours."

"That's not what I—"

"I know what you meant," Nile interrupted. "What I mean is that you look very *pink* and healthy." Nikki felt herself growing pinker by the minute. His mind wasn't on fitness, and she knew it. Nile's attention was momentarily diverted by a waiter who came to take his order. This was her chance to get him off the subject of how easily he made her blush.

Nikki waited until the waiter turned away and said, "Just now, you sounded so French, and yet when you speak English you sound more..."

Nile gave her a look that clearly said he expected her to finish. "Can't you guess?" he prompted, and he paused for a minute after Nikki shook her head. "New York."

"I wouldn't have guessed it," Nikki said. "But you do sound a little like President Roosevelt in old newsreels."

"Scratchy?" Nile sounded sarcastic.

"Dignified," Nikki said.

"If I sound that much like FDR you could have safely risked a guess. Anyway, that's my other half. You might say English was my second native tongue."

"But you live in France?"

"Mostly. Every summer we'd pack up the whole family and go to visit the relatives in Oyster Bay."

"I was there once," Nikki told him. "I saw the house at Sagamore Hill."

"You get around, don't you?" Nile said. "Oyster Bay, Paris, and here you are in Nice."

"You make me sound like a real traveler," Nikki said, "not just a tourist."

"Well, you hit the spots that count. Don't you?"

She didn't know what to make of that.

Nikki studied him. Somehow his dual nationality made him even more foreign to her and more exotic. A man who moved easily between two worlds, at home in both. Nile seemed so in command. Of himself, of every situation. As he was now.

"What about you? When you're not soaking up the sun on the Riviera, or accosting strange men on the streets of Paris, where do you live?"

"Are you going to hold that over my head for-ever?"

Nile appeared to think it over. "Yes, I think so. It gives me an enormous advantage." His brows arched over eyes that shot sapphire flashes her way. If ever a man appeared to relish his advantage it was Nile Bannerman. "But you're evading me. Where do you live, Miss Damon?"

"California," Nikki answered. "San Jose."

"Always?" Nile asked.

"No. I grew up in Alabama."

"I thought there was a drop of Southern honey in your voice. How did you get to San Jose?"

"I work for Stanhope and Considine. We make computer chips and microcircuits."

"That's what you do?" Nile sounded disbelieving.

"No, I'm on the business end. I was a project manager, but now I'm the president's assistant."

Was it her imagination, or did Nile's eyes narrow ever so slightly?

"I don't lie around soaking up the sun," Nikki said quickly. "I work. I've been with Stanhope and Considine for four years, and after Sybil promoted me, she chained me to a wall and had me work on bridge, too. Between the office and bridge tournaments I don't have time to *soak*."

There was something dawning on Nile's face, but for the life of her, Nikki couldn't tell what it was until he said, "Sybil's your boss...*she's* the president?"

"Well of course she's—" Nikki's eyes sprung wide in horror. Nile wasn't just surprised that Sybil was the president; he was surprised that the president was a woman. "You didn't think...you couldn't think..." Nikki couldn't even say it.

The jaded look that hardened Nile's eyes told her that he could—and had.

Nikki took a sharp deep breath. "Despite what you think I'm capable of, I do work for a living, and I earn every dime I'm paid," she said hotly.

In reply he bowed his head to her briefly, but he made no apology for having assumed the worst of her.

"I work like the devil at bridge, but Sybil has me playing way over my head. I don't even belong here." Nikki had no idea why it was suddenly so important to tell him this. "I'm not part of this life—" she gestured vaguely "—with hotel staff wearing costumes, and all this dressing for dinner." The beginning of a twinkle returned to Nile's eyes. Nikki's practical assessment of herself was at a low ebb, but her personal courage was high. "Obviously you do belong," she said to him. "You don't need an advantage over me, Nile. You have one already."

His eyes softened slightly as he held her gaze, and he took a long time before answering her.

"If Sybil thinks you belong here, Nikki, you do. You're in very fine company, but no one on that team would put their prestige on the line if you couldn't pull your weight."

Nikki would have sworn Nile was amazed at his own words.

As if to make up for his misjudgment of her, Nile advised her about the first team she faced, the Belgians. His sober counsel lasted only long enough for them to finish coffee. Then he shed his serious intentions the way he would shrug a cloak off his shoulders. Lively mischief twinkled in his eyes.

"I do need an advantage after all, Nikki," Nile teased her. "There are over three hundred competitors here, but most of them are men." Nikki blinked at him, sure that his laughter contained a certain edge. "What chance would I have against the most beautiful woman at the tournament if I didn't know her guilty secret?"

What chance? Every chance in the world! If he wanted one. Nikki would far rather publicly confess what she'd done in Paris than admit something more disturbing. She suspected Nile's kisses lingered sweeter in her memory than in his, and every intuition told her she ought to pretend there was no such place as Paris, no such man as Nile Bannerman.

Nikki made a move to go. She told Nile she had so much to do, studying and preparing for the first match. It was time to get to work.

"About last night," Nile whispered into Nikki's ear as he pulled back her chair, "I'm still not one bit sorry. And neither are you." She couldn't quite control her reaction, but she did avert her head. "Are you, Nikki." It wasn't even a question.

Nikki left the terrace without looking back. She was too conscious of Nile's eyes following her and certain that if she turned it would be as good as a confession.

NILE'S ADVICE on her competitors was valuable, like a secret weapon. Nikki came to the match fresh from her shower, shining hair braided into a coronet. With a cool lime-green blouse topping white slacks she looked crisp and capable, and the soft beauty of her face was offset by the severity of her hairstyle. Nikki was unaware of the contradictions in her appearance and totally unself-conscious of the effect she made.

Her rigorous mental training took over, and she was able to shut out of her mind everything but the task at hand. The hours flew.

Nikki's confidence blossomed during the day's second half. She and Sybil had perfect timing, knowing exactly when to be daring and when to tread gingerly. She played the entire day, with the other pairs splitting the sessions, and when a decisive victory was on her scorecard, Nikki was jubilant. The fears that had plagued her began to retreat.

For dinner that night Nikki dressed in a turquoise jersey, one she called a glorified T-shirt, and her white wraparound skirt. Her hair, released from the braids, fell sleekly to her shoulders. Nikki walked into the dining room buoyed with relief. She had faced her first big test and passed it.

"Let me tell you what Nikki did," Sybil was saying to the gathering. "She stole that contract from right under their noses."

"Serves them right for underestimating her," someone else said.

"Never underestimate Nikki." Why, she wondered, did Nile Bannerman always find the perfect entry line? "I suspect she has tricks up her sleeve none of us ever dreamed of."

Fortunately for Nikki, minds were too occupied with bridge to catch his innuendo. Nile gave her a slow wink that was too theatrical to be meant for her alone. One of these days, she predicted, he would tempt someone to ask what was so funny about their private joke. Nile didn't help matters by leaning close to her and growling in an audible whisper, "Just to let you know I still have the upper hand."

Nikki tried to frown but she couldn't stop the smile that came unbidden to light her face. She didn't want to respond so strongly or so readily to this handsome rogue of a man. Yet she did want to learn what lay beneath the surface of his undeniable appeal.

Nikki still had a certain wariness of him, and it wasn't only for what he might say. Nile stirred her feelings in a way she could neither dismiss nor understand. It was all backward—he kept her off balance like a fencer trying to make her drop her guard. Then, when she most needed her guard, when she would go into his arms as if nothing else in the world mattered, she would have no defence.

If only she'd just met him—here and not in Paris. If only she'd gotten to know the man inside and let him know her, before he'd turned her life topsy-turvy with those kisses that were too much, too soon.

Nikki caught the end of something Nile was saying to Sybil. "Nikki told me just this morning how much she dislikes all this dressing for dinner." What was he up to? She'd said no such thing, only that she didn't fit in with it. "If I can get her to put in an appearance at the casino tomorrow night and do her duty to the press, what say I reward her with the next night off?"

Before she knew it, Nile was in firm possession of her time, and he'd done it again, making it seem like her idea.

The evening followed the pattern of the one before. Nikki chafed through dinner, eager for the meal to end. Merely, she told herself, so she could call Nile on the carpet.

Inevitably he claimed a dance. "What was that all about?" she asked him.

To her surprise his answer struck a nerve. "A parry to your next move. Should I let you skitter away from me and pretend Paris never happened?" Nikki wondered if he could be guessing, or if he understood why her conscience demanded those feeble efforts to avoid him. "Maybe I should be a gentleman and politely ignore you."

"You won't, will you?" It was a question as well as a statement, and spoken far more wistfully than Nikki intended.

"No, rest assured I won't." Nile chuckled softly and pulled her closer. "You have definitely captured my attention, and I have but to speak a single word, and I know I'll capture yours."

While Nikki rebelled mentally against the urge to let her limbs melt into the strength of his, sweet warmth spread a velvet flush along her skin. Heart and head battled for supremacy. It was so tempting to simply yield to the music and the firm commanding pressure of his arms. She couldn't be this close to Nile and keep her senses all of a piece. They were threatening to betray her. Her hand in his responded to the way his fingers curled and to the warmth between their palms. Even her breath was treacherous. She was exquisitely sensitive to the pressure of his fingertips at her back, varying with every breath she took.

Nikki kept her eyes resolutely fixed upon the white of his shirtfront, the black of his lapels, hoping against hope that she could shut out the bronzed glow of his skin, avoid the compelling sapphire of his eyes.

She simply had to ignore his appeal. Let her head govern, not her heart. After all, anyone would be interested in such an extraordinarily attractive man. Anyone would react this way. These weren't emotions, they were only reactions. Nikki was talking herself onto firmer ground. She risked a look at him.

"How much did you win by?" Nikki asked. That was something safe to talk about.

"We blitzed," Nile replied. "They never got a plus score."

Nikki said, "Wow. It takes phenomenal play to crush a good team, and your opponents were first-rate. I am impressed."

"Are you?"

"Yes, I am."

"You're not just saying that to flatter me?"

"The devil take your hide, Nile Bannerman. I never saw anyone in my life less in need of flattering. What do you think I am?"

"Now that, I really don't know."

Nikki was surprised at how strangely honest his answer sounded, and she felt even more adrift. Had he ever been uncertain of anything in his life?

Nile held her just a little tighter and swirled her around the dance floor, humming along with the orchestra until the song was finished.

"You had a big win today yourself," he said. "And you tried to convince me you're not a master of the game."

"At this level? Day after day? Nile, there are whole books about Mr. Orsini and his team. Everybody on my team is in at least one book. *They* are masters of the game."

"I have to hand it to you, Nikki. You can really sidestep an issue," Nile said, shaking his head. Something caught his eye, and he took Nikki's hand. "Hey, look, the working press. They love to talk to a winner. Let's go get your share of the limelight for you."

Nikki tried to pull back. "I'd rather not. Those are the big bridge columnists. I wouldn't know what to say."

"Are you serious?"

"Do you know what to say to someone who writes for the international press?" Nikki looked at Nile. "I guess you would."

Nile propelled Nikki with a purposeful stride toward the group of reporters. "This," he intoned to Nikki sotto voce, "is part of your duty, and mine. Don't think of it as talking to the press. Think of it as getting publicity for your sponsor."

Nikki's "Oh" drew another, closer look from Nile. "You're right," she said. "They'll have to mention Stanhope and Considine."

"Cheer up, they won't bite. Some of them are old friends of mine."

Old friends or not, they had all the reporter's instincts. After a discussion of the toughest hands, one reporter said, "You'd make a good human interest story as the youngest player at the tournament. What do you hope to achieve?"

Nikki replied frankly. "The same thing most of us want. To get through the first series and not be bottom seed. Mr. Orsini is sure to be top, and he'll knock the bottom seed out on the first day of finals."

For this she got a sympathetic smile.

"Just keep your wits about you," one reporter advised. "It doesn't do to be terrified of your opponents."

"Nikki doesn't scare easily," Nile said, grinning. "You'd be amazed at what it takes to make her terrified of me."

"That's a different story," came the bantering reply. "It shows good judgment to be wary of a heartbreaker like you. But seriously—" and now the tone made it clear they were tending to business "—we do want to follow you through this tournament, Nikki. Will you spare some time?" Nikki readily promised that she would.

Nikki was expecting it when Nile caught her elbow and slipped her out of the ballroom, but she was completely surprised when he said, "Let's call it a night, Nikki."

She was about to protest that it was still early, but what would Nile make of that?

Nikki offered no resistance as he guided her toward the elevator and punched the button for her floor. Her regrets that the evening was over, she would keep to herself. Until now she'd known in her heart that Nile had cause to think of her as forward. She hadn't questioned why he was so determined not to let her get away.

That reporter put things in a different light with a single word: *heartbreaker*. The word hung like a barrier between them, but that, too, she would keep to herself.

Nikki was acutely aware that Nile was too vital a man to let any barrier stand for very long.

At her door she turned to him. "I'll say goodnight." Then crazily she wanted to keep him here, if only for a moment longer. "There is one thing..."

"Oh, there is?" He hadn't made a move to leave.

"We might as well get this straight." Nikki took a deep breath. "Yes, you do have the upper hand, as you so delicately put it. There are a few things I'd rather not be general knowledge." Nile arched a brow at her understatement. "But what you said to that reporter was going too far."

Nile's expression was clearly a parody of an innocent "Who, me?"

"I am *not* terrified of you. Not in the slightest, and you needn't try to make it seem that way."

"Not at all?" Nile drawled the question out.

"No!"

A smile played at the corners of his lips. "Fear doesn't play one small part in making you promise your days and nights to me?" He was daring her to deny it.

"No," Nikki said again.

"Careful now, Nikki, you don't want to give yourself away."

Too late Nikki realized the trap he'd laid for her. If she said another word, she'd give away her feelings. And they were so confused. Nikki looked at him, all her confusion written on her face. "All I mean to say is, I'm not terrified of you."

"You ought to be." Harshness edged his voice. How could a face look so soft and so hard at the same time? she wondered. Nile's features were etched in a sharp clarity that made them seem chiseled, even in the dim light of the hallway. The blue was gone from his eyes and they were black as the darkest night, swallowing her in their depths.

"You ought to be," he said again. This time the harsh edges seemed directed against himself, not her.

Before she could utter one word, Nikki was caught in the force that slowly brought her closer to that midnight gaze, and she lifted her mouth, so reluctant and yet so eager, to receive his kiss.

It was a kiss that in itself was a warning. Nile crushed her to him, and her form yielded as her words couldn't. What did it matter that she gave herself away? Caution abated, and Nikki's lips parted beneath his, urging him to plunder the sweetness of her mouth.

Nile's hands gripped her shoulders almost painfully, and he drew his thumbs along the lower edges of her clavicles, as if he sought their definition to keep him from seeking the fuller warmth below, in the swelling of her breast.

Then his fingertips slowly traced a trail of fire along the column of her throat, until they reached a spot where her pulse beat, and he pressed against the beating until Nikki felt the hammering of her heart seem to leap into his hand.

He brought his mouth again to hers. "Who was it that said, 'This way lies madness'? You can't be real." Nile's rasping whisper was so low, Nikki didn't know if she was hearing him or her own thoughts. He looked at her with the eyes of a stranger and added, "If you are even remotely what you seem to be, Nikki Damon, one of us should be running for dear life."

CHAPTER FOUR

BY THE END of the following day Nikki's thoughts were far from running for dear life. Since early morning she'd been walking on air, and the evening could only crown the day with an extra measure of happiness.

Nikki let it all flood through her mind in a series of flashes too quick to analyze. Nile joining her for a morning swim, pacing her and then daring her to follow his lead into cobalt seas struck with lozenges of golden light. The languid and sensuous matching of stroke for stroke as they swam back to shore. Nile again, water sleek and glistening, as he strode onto the beach, laughing and exuberant.

Not that he'd put aside his roguish behavior. "I've decided Sybil's policy is the one for me. I'm joining you in pursuit of a sound mind."

Who could resist a man who put on such an angelic expression while lying through his teeth about his motives? Especially when the angelic expression wavered just as Nikki took off her beach robe. Not a word about the night before.

Nikki had her own particular brand of madness. To have a sound mind where Nile was concerned, she'd have to swim all the way to China. She'd hummed beneath her breath as she followed close behind him, watching the rivulets of water trace a wandering course around his muscles.

Recollection brought a smile to Nikki's face as she pictured him on the terrace. He was just too tall for those little wrought-iron tables, and their daintiness only made her more vividly aware how masculine he looked sitting there.

He was so amused at her moment of sheer panic when Sybil joined them, announcing that Nikki was to play against France. "Oh, not yet!" It was too soon, or too late, to think of Nile as the enemy. She'd played against friends, but never against someone who meant to her—just what did Nile mean to her?

It was France Number Two, Sybil hastened to add, postponing the time when surely Nile might be Nikki's adversary. Someday, but not today.

Strangely the match itself was almost a blur. Her team was down at the half, but Sybil didn't pull her out to let her stronger teammates retrieve the match, and the vote of confidence gave Nikki a calm assurance. She emerged victorious.

Sybil's satisfied "Hah!" as she tallied up the scores, said it all for Nikki. She wasn't going to falter or give in to doubts and insecurities. She was living up to her reputation as Nikki-Nerves-of-Steel. One win might have been a lucky break—this time Nikki knew she'd earned it.

Walking on air? Nikki was dancing. After a day when everything went right, she couldn't wait for the evening.

"Wear your prettiest dress," Nile urged her, as if Nikki needed reminding that dinner at the casino meant dressing to the teeth. Before this competition was over, everyone would realize that her evening wardrobe consisted of two reversible wraparound skirts—the lights and the darks. Nikki flipped the light skirt to its silver side and paired it with a shimmering blouse of gossamer weave, the neckline becomingly shaped in a wide oval front and back.

If Nikki thought Nile would forego his taunts when they were alone, though, she was sadly mistaken. He was up to his old devilry when he commented on her dress. "Are you supposed to look like a shaft of moonlight? Or Diana the Huntress, chaste and pure? What a miserable failure." Nikki wasn't about to contradict him. Anything she said would just egg him on. "You look like a perfect peach wrapped in silver tissue," Nile continued, his voice full of mischief. "You know that, don't you, Nikki? That cool silver shine only makes the peach look more luscious, more tempting."

Just thinking that Nile found her tempting and desirable sent wild thrills coursing through her. At the same time it scared her. He always seemed to know what she was thinking.

Intuitively Nikki adopted Nile's own bantering tone. She said, "I do know," with a jaunty purr. "You told me yourself I'm your peach-and-burgundy beauty. Just watch out for the pits."

For an instant Nile was speechless. Then crescent lines appeared alongside his mouth. Nikki watched him lose the struggle to keep from laughing. Oh, wonderful, she thought, he's finally forgiven me.

Nile took her by taxi to the casino, and they shared the ride with some members of his team. Nikki's attention strayed. "Look, all along the boulevard," she said. "Glitter palaces. It's just like Disneyland." After sundown Nice was a marvel of opulence, and Nikki was eager to see it all. The ride was much too short.

A quartet of sports cars came roaring up the casino drive, and Emilio Orsini alighted from one.

"Now *there's* a sponsor," Nikki quipped. Playing for a leading Italian car manufacturer, Orsini's team was provided with sleek examples of the automotive craft. For every match they won, the car company got another headline. Nile's bridge partner asked if it made Nikki wish she were Italian.

"I don't know," Nikki answered. "My vote goes to Switzerland. All those banks. Why don't we see what their team has on display?"

"Pharmaceuticals," Nile said. "A lifetime supply of pills."

"That's too bad," Nikki said. "Their team wins and we'll think of headaches."

"How about you, Nikki?" one of their group asked.

She shrugged and said, "What can you do with computer chips?"

The French team members went into the casino, leaving Nile and Nikki outside.

"Your turn, Nile," Nikki said. "What is the House of Bannerman anyway?"

He looked at her so coldly it was all she could do not to jump back a pace.

"Come off it, Nikki," he said. "That's too much, even from you."

It was like having a steel door slammed down in front of her.

"You never told me," Nikki persisted. "Now I'm almost scared to ask. Is it something awful, like munitions?"

One corner of Nile's mouth twitched.

"Are you going to tell me or not? What's the *pièce de résistance* from House of Bannerman?"

Nile's arm shot out to expose his wrist beyond the brilliant white of his cuff, offering to view a slim silhouette of gold, brushed in the Florentine fashion, the only adornment a small raised golden *B*. "These," he said tersely.

Nikki leaned closer to have a better look. The watch was exquisite, its beauty in the perfect proportion of design. She turned to Nile. "You're a watchmaker," she said, half questioning. Obviously a good one, she thought. This was nothing ordinary, yet Nikki had never heard of Bannerman watches.

Nile made a little choking sound, but when she glanced up at him, all he did was give her one of those sharp, strange looks.

Nikki felt utterly lost, aware of undercurrents all around her. How could he expect her to know, if he didn't tell her?

"Was that so hard? Nile, you make a federal case out of everything. That's a beautiful watch, a masterpiece. From now on every time I see you, I'll think of Bannerman watches."

Did he actually start to snarl? "Of course you will, Nikki. Just the way every time I see you my mind goes racing straight to computer chips."

Nikki's eyes twinkled at him. "They have to be Stanhope and Considine chips, Nile, or it won't do any good."

Of all Nile's reactions, this was the most peculiar one she'd ever seen. He wasn't angry looking any more. He wasn't laughing. He was utterly serious.

"Nikki, what are you doing? Why are you really here?"

"To play bridge, to win as much as we can." Then she thought a minute. "Oh, I see what you mean. This business of sponsorship is really serious. I only halfway realized it." Nikki knew Sybil intended to expand her business operations into Europe, and wanted to put the firm before the public. "Somehow our team is more personal." Nikki searched for words to put her thoughts more clearly. Nile hadn't ever asked her anything serious before. "For us it was a way to test ourselves." That wasn't quite right. "To test me. Syb has put so much into me. She never once told me to promote the company. You're not either, Nile. You haven't said one word about Bannerman watches."

"Forget about the watches for a minute," Nile said.

"Okay," Nikki replied. "But if publicity is so important, how are you going to get it? Bridge isn't like tennis on television."

Nile cocked his head thoughtfully. "Okay—European bridge champions are celebrities. In some circles they're treated like royalty. There's a glamour attached to all of us." Nile frowned slightly. "If you're not aware of it by now, you soon will be. If this sponsorship experiment goes well—" He stopped in midsentence. "But think for a moment. What do you get out of this personally?" he asked suddenly.

Nikki had a ready answer. "A chance to play against the best in the world," she responded. "The excitement of something entirely new. A trip I could never take on my own, with all expenses paid." There were other, intangible things she couldn't begin to tell him.

"What do you suppose the sponsors get out of it?"

Nikki had only just begun to question this.

Nile answered for her. "How much do you think it's worth to have your company's name mentioned a dozen times in articles on the international bridge competition, in every newspaper in Europe? Doesn't some of the championship glamour rub off?"

Once again Nikki had it brought home to her just how different she was from Nile. Here she was, just beginning to feel she could justify Sybil's faith in her, and completely unaware of anything beyond that. Nile carried the double burden of playing in competition and having sponsorship of the team, but to look at him you'd think he had nothing more on his mind than the pursuit of Nikki Damon.

That pursuit was becoming less of a game and more and more puzzling with every passing hour. Nile was talking to her, really talking for the first time. He still looked every bit as much the buccaneer as the day she met him, and she didn't doubt the pirate in Nile would surface again soon. But the man's character went deeper than that—every glimpse she caught of it told her that was so.

Was this why he'd said one of them should be running for dear life? Did something in him demand that he give her fair warning? A warning that this was nothing more than an encounter, spiced by—what did he call it?—glamour.

Nikki was off in another world. She snapped back to her surroundings with a jolt. What had they been talking about? Oh, yes. "Glamour rubbing off... publicity..." From now on she would try to keep on track. She hoped the huskiness in her voice didn't reach Nile's ears. "If your team wins the championship, a lot of women might give their husbands Bannerman watches for Christmas. You could probably use the publicity, too, because frankly, Nile, I've never heard of a Bannerman watch.''

Either Nile found her comment riotously funny, or he was trying to cover up his indignation, because he laughed soundlessly, his shoulders shaking and his arm pressing against his chest as he almost doubled over.

''Heaven help me, I almost believe you,'' Nile said, recovering. ''Five more minutes and you'll convince me you've never heard of me, either.''

''Oh, Nile, I didn't mean it that way.'' Now she'd really hurt his feelings. Nikki wanted to take the sting out of it before they got caught up in the crowd inside. ''I've never been out of the United States before. Beautiful watches like these are probably famous all over Europe. Please don't think I'm so conceited, or so insular...''

That wicked, wicked look was back. ''I am constantly revising what I think of you, but *conceited* was never even close.'' What he did think he didn't say. ''Nikki, look me in the eye.''

She faced Nile, and he took both her hands in his. Even in the dim light of the portico his eyes sparkled, and he looked as if he didn't really want to speak. ''Did you really not know what House of Bannerman is?''

Nikki shook her head slowly. ''Not until you showed me the watch.''

Beneath his eyes a tiny muscle tensed. ''There is not a woman on the continent of Europe who doesn't know my name.''

''Nile...I'm not from the continent of Europe.''

He looked into her eyes for so long that she thought he was never going to speak. ''Nikki, House of Bannerman doesn't make watches. We are diamond merchants."

"You are *what*? Omigod!" An appalling thought struck her. Nikki came erect and dropped Nile's hands as if they were red-hot coals. "You really mean it. You mean...diamonds." Her hands fell, cold and empty, at her sides. "The King of Diamonds..." Nikki whispered, and she couldn't keep a bitter note from sounding. "You thought I knew it all along and was only playing coy."

Nile winced. "Of course I did. I assumed you knew it. Everyone knows it, Nikki. I just thought you had an intriguing new tactic."

"Tactic!"

"Dammit, yes. What else was I supposed to think? I've seen every approach and every come-on known to man, and I had to hand it to you—yours was the best. I was certainly willing to play along."

"You were testing me out," Nikki accused. If Nile had known her longer he'd have taken warning from the meaningful arch of Nikki's brow. "You accuse me of not telling the truth, and you don't even bother to introduce yourself properly. Just set up conclusions and watch me jump to them. Wait for the right moment to spring the trap door."

"Hold on a minute," Nile argued. "I had every reason to set a trap. I may have gone a bit too far. I may be just a little bit guilty of everything you say, but you gave me every reason in the world to do it."

He could admit his treachery and in the same breath pique her curiosity. "How does one get to be just 'a little bit guilty'?" Nikki asked sarcastically.

"I've enjoyed watching you dig yourself into a hole and then try to climb out of it."

What a beastly thing to say! "Now you wait just a minute—"

"From the very first," Nile continued, ignoring Nikki's attempt to interrupt. "When you tried to convince me you kissed me in Paris just because it was on your list of things to do." Before Nikki could argue that it was, Nile was pressing on. "I halfway believed there was a list, all right, and it was 'find Nile Bannerman in Paris and make sure he remembers me in Nice.' I just didn't remember you the way you hoped I would."

"Stop trying to wiggle out of this," Nikki said. "We aren't talking about me. We were talking about you, and how you might be just a trifle guilty. I distinctly remember," she reminded him, "that you were saying that this time you went too far."

Nile's face wore a sober expression she hadn't seen before. "All I can say in my defense is that it's finally sinking in. You are that rarest of creatures, a woman who never heard of the Bannermans. A woman—" he gave a cynical smile "—who might be captivated by my own charming self."

There was something merciless in the way he said that. It was like a secret glimpse into a private room.

Nikki looked him fully in the eye and wondered if she would ever, ever understand this man. She didn't like the way he'd amused himself at her expense, but at least he had the grace to be repentant. "Oh, Nile," Nikki said, a rush of tenderness making her voice a little breathless. "Wasn't there ever a time when you didn't suspect me?"

"Once in a while," said Nile. He didn't look at all repentant anymore. Or bitter. Or suspicious. He looked as if he thought he'd found her out. "If you're not a superb tactical planner, and you're not after the Bannerman diamonds, what are you left with?'' His smile was absolutely diabolic. "For all I know there was a list, but Nikki, you kissed me because you just plain wanted to."

"Nile!" Nikki was open-mouthed.

"Careful what you say," he cautioned. "Remember, you have such a talent for digging yourself into a hole."

He was laughing when he took her arm and went through the casino doors.

Nile escorted Nikki into a dining room that for all its brilliance couldn't begin to compete with its occupants. She'd never seen such gowns or such an array of jewels. That the women were so outnumbered by the men only made them seem that much more rare and exotic.

Periodic flashes signaled the presence of the working press. Cameras were forbidden in the gaming rooms of the casino, so photographers were busy building a portfolio of snaps to use in the coming weeks.

"Nile, look!" Nikki cried. "It's just like a masquerade."

Nile surprised her by asking, "What's your definition of a masquerade?"

"Something as fantastic as this," she answered. "Everyone looking so beautiful in the dinner jackets and the gorgeous dresses, with all the jewelry sparkling like Christmas trees. The flashbulbs going off everywhere. I see what you mean about the glamour. This makes me feel glamorous myself." Then, after a look at him, she added, "Don't you laugh at me, Nile Bannerman, I do feel glamorous."

"I'm not laughing at you, Nikki. I'm laughing at myself."

There were a couple of workmanlike interviews, and Nikki was amazed at the way reporters kept detailed records of the tournament, knowing just which hands she'd played or defended. Instead of being an ordeal, the interviews were fun. "How do they know so much about me?" she asked Nile.

"They have biographical sketches of everyone here. You may know your opponents by your notes on their bridge systems, but these reporters have notes of their own." It occurred to Nikki that she could ask to see Nile's sketch, except she didn't want anyone to know she was so interested.

Nile was in a wonderful mood and apparently enjoying her company. There wasn't anyone he didn't know, and thanks to him Nikki was really getting acquainted with some of them. Every last trace of her uneasiness was gone, and Nikki found herself in a bone-deep enjoyment of his presence. For the first time her awareness of him, running like an electric current, was a simple joy and not something to be cautious of. Just him, the experience of *him*, without having to think of it or put it into words.

Nile said something in French, and Nikki looked around to see Yvette Broussard, one of the few other women playing in the tournament. Nikki's team had defeated Yvette's team today.

The quintessential French woman, Yvette Broussard was elegant and smart, fashionable and feminine. To Nikki she was the essence of *savoir faire*. Yvette spoke warmly to Nile and charmingly to Nikki. If there were hard feelings about the loss, Nikki couldn't discern them in her manner. Yvette Broussard wore her style and sophistication as easily as she wore her Paris gown and the stunning jewelry that caught Nikki's eyes.

A very slender solid wire encircled Yvette's neck, and off to one side, as if it had just come into sizzling contact with the wire, there was a jagged bolt of lightning executed in diamonds. It was so original and so beautifully done, it drew a comment from Nikki.

"This is one of Elaine's incomparable designs," Yvette said, sending a meaningful glance Nile's way. "I had a chance to show it off at the opera in Paris a week ago," she informed Nile. He frowned a little, started to say something, Nikki noticed, but the tinkling of a chime interrupted him.

Yvette wandered away to find her dinner partner, and Nikki watched her go, struck again by the elegance of her gown, the fashionable asymmetry of her hairstyle. "She didn't buy that necklace from you, did she?" Nikki asked Nile, wondering why Yvette would expect him to take an interest in where she'd shown off her dazzling diamonds.

"Nikki, I don't sell jewelry. I deal in stones. My customers are firms, like Cartier." Nile chuckled at her. "You have heard of Cartier, haven't you?"

"Wipe that look off your face, Nile Bannerman. Everybody's heard of Cartier." She started to smile. "Even those who aren't from the continent of Europe." Hah! He could look a bit abashed, given the proper nudge.

"*Touché,*" he whispered, with a half salute. "To answer your question, no, Yvette didn't buy that necklace from me. But I do have an interest in it. I selected the stones."

"Hmm." Nikki thought about this for a minute. "You must be good friends, then, if you went to that much trouble."

"I've known Yvette for years." He didn't elaborate. "I didn't choose the stones for her. I'd seen Elaine's design drawings, so I made a point of finding some good small diamonds. It was pure chance that Yvette bought the necklace."

"Oh." Then how, Nikki wondered, did Yvette know Nile had anything to do with it? She knew she hadn't mistaken the slightly conspiratorial expression on Yvette's face. Or was it that Yvette knew Nile had something to do with... "Do you often see Elaine's drawings?" she asked. Nile wasn't the only one who could be crafty.

"Most of them," Nile answered. "She did the watches for the team—at least, the case designs."

So that was the connection. Nikki's eyes were a little brighter. "She works for you."

Nile shrugged a semi-confirmation, semi-denial. "Only in the vaguest way," he said. "Hurry now. I see a couple of empty places next to Mrs. Considine."

He settled himself between Nikki and Sybil, and for a while Nikki couldn't find fault with his behavior. She was beginning to think he'd reformed. But when she remarked that her palate must be getting jaded if she could think, "Oh, no, not another cream sauce" Nile cocked his head disarmingly.

"You can see," he said to Sybil, "why Nikki is so eager to have me take her away from all this."

Sybil was smothering a grin.

Nikki edged her foot to the side and tapped Nile's shoe. She might have known he had an ulterior motive in wanting to sit by Sybil.

"She's so wise to seek my counsel, don't you think? She wants to make a list of things to do in Nice."

Sybil burst out laughing. Nikki kicked his shin.

The man just wouldn't quit. "Does Nikki seem like the type to make a list? It seems so deadly dull."

Sybil got herself together long enough to say, "It's only deadly on the feet. I should know. She *does* make lists." Nikki lunged forward to scowl at Sybil. She knew darn well Sybil got the point and was just playing along with Nile. "In fact, I think I still have one, stuck in my billfold."

"Could I see it?" Anyone who thought that was an innocent question would have to be tone deaf.

Nikki reached for the folded paper Sybil was offering, but Nile snatched it away. "I just want to be sure I'm familiar with your taste, Nikki," he said.

His now-I-have-you-in-my-clutches expression faded slowly as he scanned the top of the page where, under the corporate letterhead, was engraved, "Nicole Damon, Assistant to the President." The list was neatly typed, orderly, complete with notes like "closed on Tuesdays." It could have been a business document, except that at the bottom, in Nikki's freely flowing script, was written "April in Paris" and more.

"I think I'll hold on to this," Nile said, slipping the list into his pocket. Throughout the meal he was as charming as ever and not quite so ready to provoke her. Nikki wondered what was in his thoughts.

The banquet hall was set off from the gaming rooms. While others bustled on, Nikki pulled Nile aside.

"I can't really blame you for wanting to find out if I knew who you were," she said in a tone that was meant to let him know she forgave him. "But I could throttle you for getting Sybil on your side."

"Don't I need help?" he said innocently.

"Hah! You need help like I need a—" When would she ever learn?

"Give the devil his due, Nikki. You came out of the blue in Paris, and you seemed to know me. Then here you were again."

"Stalking my prey?" Nikki asked. In spite of herself she was about to giggle, and she had to suppress it.

"Ah, Nikki," Nile said with a renegade smile, "I was willing to be stalked."

What a scoundrel. "You are impossible!"

"And you, rare creature, are improbable."

"Rare indeed. After what you've put me through, I feel well-done."

"Oh, you are, Nikki." His voice matched exactly the spark in his eyes. "You're very, very well-done."

He could make all the sport he wanted, Nikki decided. She'd seen his face when he realized she hadn't lied about the list. From now on he'd have to look at her through different eyes.

"Come along, creature, let's have a go at the games of chance."

CHAPTER FIVE

NIKKI WAS astonished. Before her eyes a scene she'd witnessed in a dozen films came to life. "Nile, look at this. It's like theater, only we're on the stage." Low-hanging lamps spilled pools of light onto bright green tabletops, and the air was thick with an almost tangible murmur of voices, unaccountably more hushed than silence would have been, and she could hear the click of chips, the whir of a roulette wheel and the calls of the croupiers. "This is so make-believe," she said to Nile. "I wouldn't be surprised to see James Bond step up and say 'Banco.'"

"Shh," Nile said quickly, and gently covered her mouth with his fingers. Without knowing it Nikki returned the pressure in a fleeting kiss. "If I were you, I wouldn't say that word out loud. You might have to make good on it."

They wandered through the room, Nikki fascinated by the gambling apparatus and Nile explaining the principle of the games. "Are you going to play?" Nile asked.

Soon. Nikki had set aside twenty dollars for the evening at the casino. Nile's brows twitched, and the corners of his mouth turned down, he was trying so hard not to laugh. "Twenty whole dollars? I can see this is really serious business to you."

"Deadly serious," Nikki intoned, catching his mood and making a mock-tragic face. "If I lose it, I can't pay the rent."

Nile grinned at her and leaned so near, the warmth of his body engulfed her. "You're such wonderful fun when you finally do let go," he said. Funny, she'd been thinking the same thing about him.

"Come on," Nile said, "let's get some chips. A big-time player like you must be ready for some action." They headed for the cashier's cage. Sybil was just ahead of them, chatting with Yvette Broussard.

"Nikki!" Sybil gestured her nearer. "Over here." They formed a line. "Yvette's going to teach me to gamble."

"I shouldn't, after today," Yvette said, turning smoothly to Nile. "These partners, when they play against you—watch out for them. This one—" she pointed to Sybil "—has won the Venice Cup, and this one—" pointing to Nikki "—fears no man."

Sybil backed her up. "Nerves of steel," she said.

A voice came from nearby. "Are those American accents? It's unusual to hear them so early in the season." Nikki turned. A man stood almost at her shoulder, speaking with a pleasant, though coolly reserved manner. He was polite, Nikki thought, and not trying to intrude. Sybil made a quick and gracious reply, to which the man responded, "Please don't think me forward, but I couldn't help overhearing."

Nikki flashed a rapid data-gathering glance at the man. He was pleasant enough to look at, with very fair hair and pale eyes of aquamarine. He was continuing. "Are you enjoying your stay in Nice? What brings you at this time of year?"

He went on to introduce himself as Paul Moray, a yacht salesman, and manners demanded the others introduce themselves in turn. Nikki noticed his hands, slim and deft and particularly well cared for. His fair brows quirked when he was introduced to Nile. Nikki he favored with a fleeting glance and soon dismissed. He wasn't immune, though, to the other women.

Sybil was wearing a dress that made the gaming tables a pale imitation of the color green. Even Nile had complimented her, and rightly so. Yvette's regal style was a masterpiece of design.

Nikki sensed a tension in Nile, and it puzzled her to see a frown pulling his brows downward. She followed his eyes and found him studying Moray. Curious, she tried to see what bothered him.

All she could detect was Moray's interest in Yvette and Sybil, but clearly it was Yvette who interested him most. As Moray chatted, though, Nikki decided he was simply hell-bent on charming the ladies, and was more at home with a French woman than an American. He offered another polite welcome to Nice and wished them well at the bridge tournament.

Nikki was next at the cashier's cage. In seconds she'd exchanged her money for a few chips and was ready to go with Nile.

With a slight frown of consternation Nikki held her hand palm up, displaying the chips. "This certainly isn't much—" The sight of Nile's face stopped her in midsentence. His eyes were veiled and distrustful, lending him a saturnine look.

"Nile?" she ventured.

"What? Oh." The glacial look was still on his face. "What did you think of that man?"

What man? Nikki was about to say, when she remembered the way Nile had looked at Paul Moray. "Oh, him," she said, dismissing the stranger entirely. Nikki hadn't said a word all through the brief encounter. "He certainly has an eye for the ladies."

"He has too much of an eye," Nile said, the sound of bitter gall in his voice.

Jealousy? Nikki wondered, all the while doubting it. Nile Bannerman was no man to be plagued by jealousy, of that she was certain. He was too sure of himself, and that assurance went all the way to the marrow of his bones.

"Come off-it," Nikki said with genial severity. "He only had eyes for Yvette, anyway." She hoped to tease him out of this mood.

Surprisingly Nile responded, "That's what I'm afraid of." He had yet to look her in the eye, instead was following someone with his gaze—Nikki assumed it must be Paul Moray. "Excuse me a minute," he said in a distracted tone.

His long stride quickly caught him up to Yvette and Sybil, and Nikki watched him take Yvette aside. They were so . . . so *French* . . . the way they gestured as they talked. Nile seemed to be emphasizing some point, and Yvette brushed it aside, her eloquent shrug just the beginning of a graceful sweep of her expressive hands.

If Nile cautioned Nikki like that, she'd certainly pay him more heed. Nikki could almost hear the "Nooo, nooo" from Yvette's pursed lips. What was the woman thinking?

What was Nile doing?

A strange feeling began to creep over Nikki. Here she stood in the most worldly place she'd ever been, rubbing shoulders with the Beautiful People, and she was like a kid with her allowance in her hand. There Nile was, in plain view, carrying on a heated exchange with Yvette. And he'd just told Nikki he didn't like Yvette being the object of another man's attention.

Nikki shook her head sharply. Suspicions. She was getting to be just as bad as Nile. Well, she wouldn't jump to any conclusions. But . . .

Nile was coming back. "Is there some trouble?" Nikki asked, when he reached her side.

"It may be nothing at all," he said obliquely. He was still frowning. "The trouble was in Paris." Evidently it was present in his mind. "Yvette is just too devil-may-care."

He sounded thoroughly put out, and Nikki felt relieved when he turned to her suddenly and flashed a smile. "Where were we?" he said, adding, "Oh, yes." Nile picked up her hand and held her palm before him. "The family fortune," he said, directing her attention to the pitifully few chips she held. "How did you decide on twenty dollars?" he asked, as if his disagreement with Yvette had never occurred.

She replied as easily as she could, "Ten seemed too chintzy, and fifty was way too much. Twenty is all I can afford to lose."

"Ah, Nikki." He didn't sound condescending, but Nikki could imagine how wretchedly insignificant twenty dollars would be in Nile Bannerman's scheme of things.

She asked him, "Don't you ever set limits on how much you're willing to lose?"

"I don't expect to lose," Nile answered her. "Not ever, not anything." His face clouded again, and he seemed very far away.

It took some effort for Nile to break that strange mood, Nikki noticed, but he accompanied her to the gaming tables, nevertheless, and gave her a short summary of how to play. Nikki chose her table, and just to be sure she understood what Nile taught her, she observed a few games without betting. More players were coming to the table, and Nile whispered that she must play or yield her place to someone else.

Nikki had seen enough. There were two decks of cards in play, and for Nikki it was just like keeping track of two bridge hands simultaneously.

Cautiously she wagered one token. There was a barely perceptible movement from Nile standing beside her. The corner of her eye caught the way his glance flickered past her head and away from her. She looked the other way. On the other side of her, appearing totally indifferent to her presence, was Paul Moray.

The game progressed, but Nikki was so quickly out of the competition that she paid more attention to the crowd than to the cards flying from the dealer's hands.

Across the table something caught her eye. The light bathing the table illuminated the players but left their faces half in shadow. Directly opposite Nikki the light struck sparks from a diamond bolt of lightning, and she realized that the slender arm placing chips belonged to Yvette Broussard.

Nikki followed the deal around the table until it passed her by. For a moment she took in the face of the fair-haired man beside her. The yacht salesman wasn't following the action of the dealer or paying attention to the fall of the cards. He was staring straight at Yvette.

Hastily Nikki caught up with the dealer's progress, all the while feeling a wariness emanating from Nile at her left side. The game was over quickly, and after raking in the chips, the dealer began another round. Nikki wagered more tokens and tried to return her attention to the game, but the feeling never left her that Nile was very much on edge.

Across the table Yvette gathered in her chips and vanished from the pool of light. Seconds later Paul Moray vacated his spot. His going brought on a tension in Nile that Nikki could literally feel, a tension that nearly tore him from her side. It lasted until the other man vanished from the casino, and then Nile began to relax bit by bit into the ease and all-pervasive warmth that Nikki had come to associate with him.

For reassurance Nikki studied Nile's face. His eyes, even in the half-light above the glare of the table lamp, were once again as clear as a summer sky. For all his rakish daring and his dangerous looks, he had eyes that were lit from within. Was that the secret of Nile's vividly wicked appeal? A quality of light, something so elusive she couldn't even pin it down?

Looks were strange, Nikki thought. Rogue, pirate, scoundrel, renegade. She'd used every one of those words to describe Nile, but she had only to look at him to know he would never do her harm. Yet that bland, blond man who'd just left was another story entirely. For some reason Nile might be capable of harming him, Nikki thought as she turned her attention to the game.

This time the dealer was in a dangerous position. Nikki had been carefully counting cards as they were played, and the ones outstanding gave her an excellent chance to win. Rewarded for her effort, she raked in a big pile of chips. On the next round Nikki was even more attentive. The dealer was very fast, but when her time came to wager or fold, Nikki took a little time to think. What could give her a chance? There weren't many cards unknown. Nikki figured the odds and upped her bet.

Another win. On the next hand three flint-eyed men stood beside the dealer, watching Nikki. The dealer was under visible stress. At each of her turns Nikki paused to scan the cards and implant them firmly in her memory. This time the pile of chips she won was smaller and a different color. Nile told her they were worth much more.

A moment's delay and the dealer was replaced with another. Casino patrons tried to reach the table, but the three men with their frozen countenances refused to move.

The next game was a repeat of the previous one. The new dealer had a rhythmic flick of the wrist and snapped the cards to make them fly around the table with dazzling speed. Some of the players left the game. The new dealer had no better luck. For three hands in a row the stick had pushed a pile of chips Nikki's way. An excited murmur, the first she'd really heard, flowed around the table.

At once the three figures deserted the dealer and made their way toward Nikki. "Mademoiselle," said one of the gimlet-eyed men as he approached. "Please cash in your chips. We must ask you to leave the casino."

"What's wrong?" Nikki asked. "Has something happened?"

"We do not allow professional gamblers to play at these tables," the man said to her, briskly raking together her chips and stacking them.

"Of all the nonsense!" Nikki exclaimed. "What makes you think you can..."

The man, ignoring Nikki, turned to Nile and said, "She is a card counter. You understand, we have the right to bar her from this casino."

Nikki automatically turned to Nile, just as the man had done, to put *her* case to him. To her amazement he appeared contrite. "It's all right, Nikki. I'll explain it. Just do as the man says." He helped her carry the chips to the cashier's cage. She stuffed a wad of bank notes into her purse, and with a scowl on her face she let Nile lead her from the casino. He summoned a taxi and, as they waited, answered Nikki's demand to know what on earth had made those—those bouncers think she was a professional gambler. "You were counting, weren't you Nikki?"

"Of course I was. How else can you tell when to bet?"

Nile threw back his head and laughed, a sound of pure delight. "And you were doing very well," he added. "That was your downfall. Professional gamblers are card counters, but they don't make it obvious." He gave her a conspiratorial nudge. "If you could learn to be a little more subtle, you could break the bank."

"Hah!" Nikki said, but she was beginning to find the situation funny. Not many people had the dubious distinction of being thrown out of a casino.

"You think you couldn't do it?" Nile asked. "Do you know how much you just stuffed into your purse?" Nikki shook her head. "A little over twelve hundred dollars." Nikki's jaw dropped. "Not bad for a few minutes' work. You can see why they wouldn't want you dropping in night after night."

"But I wouldn't," Nikki said. "If it's all that easy to win, I'd soon get bored."

Even richer laughter spilled from Nile's throat, and it was contagious. "Are you the girl with the careful plan not to lose more than twenty dollars?"

"That was before I found out I was a professional gambler," Nikki said. "Well," she said flippantly, "that's one world conquered. Where do we go from here?"

"Monte Carlo," Nile offered. "The night is young, and they've never heard of you there."

"We could be out of France by morning and retire forever on my winnings."

"We?"

"Sure," said Nikki. "I'm generous to a fault. At last, Nile, you can quit the diamond business and go to a desert island where no one's ever heard of you."

Nikki's sides were aching as she stepped into the taxi, and she brushed at the corner of her eye. Once inside she said to Nile in a voice still weak with laughter, "That's really such a dumb thing to do with money."

From the driver's seat came a voice. "Don't cry lady. Everyone has bad luck sometimes."

"Owww," Nikki wailed, about to start laughing all over again, and she turned her face into Nile's chest to muffle the sounds. Nile put an arm around her, tight, and she could hear a rumble deep in his chest and feel the way his shoulder muscles tensed as he held back an outburst of his own.

He said to the driver, "It was only twenty dollars. She takes things awfully hard."

NILE HAD the driver drop them on the boulevard in front of the hotel. By unspoken agreement they walked to the beach, now deserted in the darkness, and found one of the padded cushions for a seat.

There was no light but the moon and the reflection of it now and then on a breaking wave. A breeze caught Nikki's silver dress, and it fluttered in the moonlight. Of Nile she could see only the white triangle of his shirtfront and his face, shadowed but distinct.

Nikki had a strange suspended feeling. She hadn't ever really come face-to-face with Nile. Always he'd been hidden behind a mask, one of his own making that he'd held in front of her. Only tonight had the mask begun to come down.

How many secrets had it hidden? It stung Nikki to think that Nile had believed, even for a minute, that her response to him could be just a tactic. Then she thought again of how often women must have thrown themselves into his arms and not always, as he put it, for his own charming self.

Who was the man behind the mask? Would he have the same power to stir her? More?

Nile was leaning on his elbow, making room for Nikki beside him. The curve of his arm beckoned but Nikki wouldn't curl into that inviting embrace. One look, one touch, and it would be too late for talk.

"Don't you think it's time you filled in some of the gaps?" she asked him, hoping that she sounded just tart enough to hide the depth of her feeling.

"Gaps?"

"All the things you thought I knew about you. Bannerman's probably your real name. You're in the wholesale business. You live in Paris. I only knew one out of three."

"Wrong. I live in Neuilly."

"Where's that?" Nikki asked.

"A suburb of Paris."

"Same thing."

"No it isn't, Nikki. If you'd done your homework..."

The pale wash of moonlight cast dark shadows on Nile's face, but there was light enough to see him realize what he'd said, and to see the jolt it gave him.

"If I'd done my homework... I'd know who R. N. Bannerman is," Nikki said quietly. "What does the *R* stand for?"

His voice deepened. "Robert," he said, but his answer was automatic. His thoughts seemed to be elsewhere.

"Is Nile a family name?"

He shifted a bit, sitting up beside Nikki, and once more sounded like himself. "There was a Scotsman named Bannerman who married the daughter of Elias Nile, a diamond merchant in New York and Oyster Bay. The names get switched around a bit, but they're tacked onto someone in some form or other in every generation. The occupation is voluntary."

Nikki said, "I like it. The name," she added.

"How about Elias?"

"I'd have to think about that. It sounds awfully rocky and forbidding. Is there an Elias?"

Nile groaned audibly. "You have a deserted beach and the moon over the water, and you want to waste it talking about my relatives?"

"What would you rather talk about?" Nikki asked.

"The good old days."

"What good old days?"

"The days when you'd rather do anything than have me talk."

Nikki smiled. The night wind was damp so near the water, and she shivered a little. Nile took off his jacket and put it around her shoulders. Then he drew her to her feet. "I know just the thing to warm you up. We'll have a brandy." He walked her back to the hotel at a pace that left her breathless. "You've already gotten me thrown out of one place tonight. We won't chance the public rooms. Come with me."

Before Nikki could say a word, Nile brought her around the terrace and unlocked the door to a cabana suite. Nikki hesitated at the door. "Come on inside," Nile urged her. "Throw that jacket on the chair."

Nikki stepped into a small sitting room with easy chairs and a tiny bistro table. Nile opened a bar cabinet on the wall to get two snifters, and as he poured a small amount of brandy into each, Nikki glanced around. The suite was furnished even more richly than her room in the main hotel. Nile had stacks of bridge notes on the table, and the sight of them made her feel at home. She picked up a set at random and settled into a chair as Nile handed her the brandy glass.

The pages were worn and dog-eared, headed by the word, *"Suisse."* She knew Nile was playing Switzerland tomorrow. "This is all in French," she said.

Nile's face creased in amusement. "What did you expect? We're a French team." He shuffled through the other piles of notes. "You're in here somewhere," he said. "Here." He handed her another set of papers.

"États Unis Deuxième," Nikki read. "Mmm, we sound so formidable in French."

"Keep going," Nile said, loosening his tie and settling into a chair opposite her.

Nikki read aloud, faltering where she was unsure of a word. Her knowledge of the material helped, and soon her reading was smoother, but still slow. Frequently she glanced up at Nile to find his eyes intent upon her, and a questioning softness in his gaze quickened her pulse and brought a new note into her voice. She hesitated.

"Go on," he said. "You have a beautiful voice."

Nikki read on, the dry and concise presentation of her bidding system sounding majestic, almost seductive, in the foreign tongue. Feeling self-conscious, she no longer looked up at him.

At the end of the page Nikki halted in midsentence, raising questioning eyes to Nile. A hint of a smile played about his lips. "How was that?" she asked.

"Your accent is atrocious," Nile answered.

"You said—"

"I said your voice is beautiful, and it is. Listening to you is like listening to music. I could do it all night, even if I never understood a word you said."

In Nile's voice was a quality that made Nikki feel the same way. It had nothing to do with words.

Nikki raised the brandy snifter to her lips and took a tiny sip, her eyes never leaving his face. Nile's glass rested untouched on the table.

"There's something else I'd like you to do," he said, getting up to retrieve a folded paper from his dinner jacket. He opened it and handed it to her. "Read this to me, Nikki."

Not knowing quite what Nile expected, Nikki took the paper. At first she was merely reading, ticking off the items rapidly, one by one, and glancing over the top of the page at Nile, sprawled like a lazing cat across from her as she read. He listened intently, with a slight narrowing of his eyes and an inclination of his head, as if he could see the list himself, as she named each item.

Nikki didn't have to look farther down the page to remember. She let her hand with the paper drop into her lap.

Was this what he wanted to know? That it really wasn't a made-up story? Unconsciously she was slowing down, reciting from memory, and the last few phrases she spoke directly to him. The power of his gaze, the way his eyes held hers, made it so difficult to breathe. She couldn't help the catch in her voice or the way it dropped to a whisper when she said, "April in . . . Paris."

Before Nikki could put down the page Nile was on his feet and pulling her from her chair. Her silver skirt crinkled as he crushed her against his chest.

How willingly she fell into his arms, returning his hungry kisses force for force. In the quiet room she could hear the pounding of her heart, urging her to forget, let him forget, the doubts and the clouded beginning. This was for now, for him, and not for an unknown stranger.

Was she a stranger to him still? For a moment he pulled away, and when he brought his mouth to hers again, it was like the time in Paris. Soft, fleeting touch, and then a kiss that deepened slowly, as if the touch and taste of her were something new.

"You haven't told me everything." Nile's husky whisper was near her ear. Nikki was breathless and unsteady, her pulse racing. Nile asked her, "In your fantasy, after you kissed your Frenchman, what happened then?"

Nikki murmured, "I walked away into the sunset. He smiled an enigmatic smile."

Nile looked at her, the ghost of a tantalizing smile on his lips. "Was it like this?" he teased her.

"I don't remember anymore," Nikki answered truthfully. "I can't remember him at all. I remember you."

If Nikki's heart was racing before, now it was wild in her breast. What was written in Nile's eyes, she mirrored inside, and the force of it made her tremble and back away from him. She couldn't stay another minute in his arms.

Nikki couldn't decipher the look on his face as he asked, "Are you going to walk away into the sunset now?"

"Nile, I . . . I have to."

Nile's fingers raked through his dark unruly curls. "Are you playing games, Nikki? If you are, you're only doing it for yourself. I don't need them."

How easily he could bruise her with his cynicism. "Nile, you don't understand anything about me."

His jaw tightened. "You're right, Nikki. I don't. But do you understand me any better? Do you have to?" He spun around away from her, and Nikki could hear his breath, deep and swift, sharply exhaled. "Brandy wasn't such a good idea, was it, Nikki? I'd better take you home."

CHAPTER SIX

THE EVENING seemed so unfinished, but it was coming to an abrupt end. Nikki was no more willing than Nile was to say another word as he took her to her room. Couldn't he see what was happening to her? She dared not let herself be swept into the current of her emotions, or even examine them very carefully. They were too bewildering.

When had the man of fantasy disappeared and Nile, with all his suspicions, taken his place? No wonder he didn't understand her. Nikki wasn't sure she understood herself.

He gave her no clue as he unlocked the door for her and said, "Good night, Nikki."

She was the one with regret in her voice when she said good-night. Nile pushed the door open and had turned away before she was inside.

The next day he was absent when Nikki showed up for her swim, and she was more than disappointed. Now it was just another early morning. Without Nile the zest was missing.

Nikki was later than usual when she headed for breakfast at her customary table on the terrace. There she saw Nile waiting, and her first sight of him made her apprehensive. They'd both had time for second thoughts about what was happening between them, and it appeared Nile's thoughts were not the same as hers.

Nile wore a dark expression, too somber to belong on the sun-drenched terrace, and to Nikki it was a poor omen for the day. She made her way to the table, while heads turned and conversation lulled as she walked by, to buzz again immediately when she passed. It was hard to say which was more disturbing, the frank stares or the expression on Nile's face.

He appeared restless, and beneath his eyes were the shadows of what might have been a sleepless night. "I want to have a word with you," he said, and from his tone Nile's dilemma was apparent to Nikki. He both did and didn't want to see her.

Nikki felt hampered by the presence of so many people, all of whom seemed to be staring her way. Nile must see them, too, she thought. He was scanning the terrace, looking annoyed.

"Should we go somewhere else?" Nikki asked.

She thought he was tempted, but he only said, "No, the damage is done already. We might as well stay here."

Damage? Nikki recoiled from so strong a word.

Nile put a folded newspaper on the table. "Would you like to practice your French translation some more?" he asked.

"So you can laugh at my accent?"

"I won't laugh," Nile replied tersely. "Not today. There's an article in here you'll find particularly...interesting."

"What is it?" she asked, mystified by Nile's tone of voice.

"You can't miss it."

She would have to study the headlines carefully. French idioms were difficult for her, and French journalese could be next to impossible.

Nikki gasped. Before she'd fully opened up the paper there was no doubt what Nile meant for her to see.

When had those photographs been taken? Nikki, usually camera-shy, had been caught unaware. Eyes sparkling, she was smiling up at someone, delight shining on her face. In Nile's photograph he wore that vividly appealing look she knew so well. The look of the buccaneer at the moment when he seized his prize.

The pictures were printed facing one another. Someone had done a clever job of framing them in playing cards, but just in case the meaning wasn't clear, they were captioned. Beneath Nile's photograph she read "The King of Diamonds," and beneath her own, "The Queen of Hearts?"

So *that* was what had him all out of sorts! Prepared for the worst she began to read the story.

When she had finished, Nikki looked up, distraught at the veiled hints the article contained. There was a scowl on Nile's face.

Nile had been described with economy of phrase, in bold outline that told Nikki he'd been written about before. She had a hard time recognizing herself in their depiction of "Nicole Damon" even though not one false word was printed. Nikki supposed, though, that anyone would seem extraordinary when the special highlights of her life were condensed.

The facts she couldn't argue. She and Nile *were* frequently seen together. It wasn't that statement that bothered Nikki. It was the question unasked but implied.

The Queen of Hearts. Was Nikki Damon Nile Bannerman's latest romance?

Small wonder every eye on the terrace had been on her. With a juicy tidbit like that in the morning paper, who could resist a little gossip?

"That's only the local paper," Nile said severely. "No doubt it will be in *Paris-Match* tomorrow. Damn newspapers!" Nile was more disturbed than Nikki had imagined. "You'd think by now I'd be immune to this." Perhaps he ought to be immune, considering how little it took to suggest he'd been written about, just this way, before. "You don't even have to give interviews to have every move—" Something stopped him in the middle of his thoughts, and he got up from the table.

"Where are you going?" Nikki asked.

"To call Paris. Are you coming?"

One thing was certain. Nikki wasn't going to stay here on the terrace and be a target for staring eyes. She doubted that even Nile could persuade a Paris newspaper not to print the article, but she was curious about how he'd try to do it.

He found a bank of telephones near the lobby, told the operator to charge the call to his suite and dialed a number without even consulting the directory. He waited for the ring.

"*Bonjour.* Elaine Bannerman, *s'il vous plaît.*"

A cold fist knotted in Nikki's stomach. Time froze, endless seconds ticking by while her mind remained empty. Nikki was pleading silently to let it remain empty. Anything was better than to be conscious of... *Elaine Bannerman!* a voice in Nikki's head was shrieking, and her cheeks flamed against the sudden pallor in her face. It was the one thing she'd never thought of, not even when Nile had been so angry about the pictures, not even when his first thought had been to call Paris.

He turned and glanced at her, the devil incarnate behind his handsome face. The icy lump of betrayal within her turned to steaming fury that he dared assume—

"Nikki? What is it?"

Nikki's teeth were clenched—to hold back all she would have said to him. Eyes blazing, she turned and walked away.

"Just a minute," she heard him say into the phone, and then he called out, "Nikki!" She kept walking. The receiver crashed down, and Nile quickly caught up with her.

"What are you doing?"

"Go back to the telephone, Nile," she said, barely able to control her voice. "Do the decent thing and make that call."

"What decent thing?" Nile grabbed her elbow, but Nikki snatched her arm away.

"How could you?" Nikki said in a tortured voice. "How could you make me a part of anything like this?"

"What are you talking about?"

Her voice was hollow as she said, "No wonder you didn't want to talk about your relatives. How convenient for you, that you neglected to mention Elaine Bannerman."

Nile looked as if she'd struck him a blow. Color drained from his face. "Good Lord," he whispered. "Elaine."

"Yes," Nikki fairly spat at him. "What a pity you didn't think of her sooner."

"Is that what you think?" His eyes grew cold as ice fields. "That I'm married and cheating?" His features were immobile, his mouth a bitter slash.

"What am I to think?" Nikki asked. "That it's a matter of a technicality? Don't try to explain to me," she added hastily. "You owe your explanations to your wife."

A deep twitch marred the corner of his mouth. "I owe an explanation to no one," he said forcefully. "There are no technicalities." Then, just as forcefully, "Elaine came by her name the same way I did mine—she's my sister."

"Do you expect me to believe that?" Nikki asked. It sounded like the most obvious lie in the world.

"It's the truth," Nile said. "How did you ever get the idea she was anything else?"

"From you, seeing her designs, and saying she worked for you only in the vaguest way." She blinked hard and clenched her fists, to keep from crying. "From Yvette, dropping her name last night, and giving you that knowing look."

Nile looked exasperated. "So you put two and two together, and came up with five."

"I had good reasons," Nikki countered.

Nile shook his head. "Come with me right now. I'm going to teach you some arithmetic." He dragged her to his suite.

When he made the second call, Nikki was a reluctant audience. "Elaine," she heard him say. "Go to the newspaper office for me. Find the article about the bridge tournament. See exactly what it says about Yvette Broussard." Nikki wondered what the newspaper had to say about Yvette that Nile couldn't ask her himself. "And find that photograph of Yvette and you together at the opera. Call me this afternoon and tell me what you learn."

Nikki raised an eyebrow at him and deliberately gave him a beady stare. What did he think he was proving?

Nile motioned her closer to the phone and aimed the receiver at her.

"Am I your favorite brother, Elaine?" he said into the mouthpiece.

"You're so funnee. You're my only brother," came a voice into the air.

"One more thing. Who were you named for?"

There was a little pause. "Nile, have you been drinking?"

"You know me better than that. Come on, Elaine. My honor is at stake."

Clear laughter came across the miles. "Too bad for you. I was named for a princess in a fairy tale, unlike my Aunt Eliza." Elaine hung up on him before he could say another word.

He didn't have to. Elaine's banter was reproach enough to Nikki. Sheepishly she hung her head. She wouldn't admit it, either, if she'd been named for a man called Elias.

"Now do you believe me?" There was still a trace of bitterness in Nile's expression, and something very puzzling in his eyes. "Nikki... Did you really mean to walk away, and just keep going?"

She nodded.

"Because of Elaine... Bannerman?"

Nikki said, "I have a low flash point where some things are concerned."

"With a flash point that low, you could at least have waited for something I'd said outright, not something you pieced together from assumptions."

Nikki deserved his indignation, and she knew it, but the pain of his imagined betrayal was just as sharp as if it were real. "When have you made a point of saying things outright?" she asked.

Nile said, "From now on, Nikki, I'll be careful not to leave things to your imagination. Before it starts working overtime again, I'd better tell you this—I'm completely unencumbered."

He put it so strangely Nikki had to think a minute before she absorbed what Nile was saying. There was no Mrs. Bannerman.

Nile was free! And it mattered, oh, so much. Nikki's heart grew lighter, and her face took on an effervescent glow.

"So am I," she said.

"I wouldn't have it any other way."

All was so right with the world.

"CONGRATULATIONS," someone called out as Nikki walked down the glass-walled hall to meet Nile. She'd had a big win, playing well despite the morning's bad start, when crisis had piled upon crisis.

Her hair was freshly braided, and she wore a sweater against the salt air breeze. She caught sight of Nile and almost ran the last few yards. His arms made a small, involuntary movement, as if to open wide, but he checked the motion and swung around shoulder to shoulder with Nikki. That small gesture, even though quickly controlled, made her inordinately happy.

They passed Yvette and a group of players who were headed for another night on the town. Yvette asked them to come along.

"We're persona non grata," Nile said. "There aren't many casinos that will let Nikki in." He hurried Nikki away before she could explain.

"Where are we going, that will let me in?"

"You'll see."

In a little open roadster he drove them to a road just above the harbor. They left the car and took a trail, partially overgrown and meandering along a hillside. Nikki fell back, to study Nile unobserved. He climbed to a spot where the ground leveled off and stood, gazing over the water.

The light of a maritime sunset tinted the sky coral and vermilion and touched Nile's face with a gentle lambency that intensified the blue of his eyes, as it did the blue of the sea.

On his face was an expression so rare, so happy, it took her breath away. To see him now made Nikki think there was something he kept hidden inside, and that only in unguarded moments did he set it free.

She stopped so long that Nile called back to her, "Hurry, or you'll miss the sunset." He beckoned her farther along the trail.

Nikki cast her gaze down rather than have him discover what seeing him in his unguarded moments did to her. She hurried up beside him.

Nile placed Nikki in front of him and held her shoulders. The colors of the day played across a veil of cloud at the western horizon. Nikki faced a sun grown huge and red, and the solar fires were nothing but a mirror of the flame that kindled in her heart.

Nile took her hand suddenly, and they raced the dying light to the bottom of the trail.

They drove to an unassuming waterfront café. The building, old and ramshackle, had been added to over the years. The original part was floored in small white hexagonal tiles, a cross between a bistro and a workingman's café, with a little bit remaining of a zinc bar along one wall. Nile led Nikki through it to a window-walled and plank-floored section where tables abutted the windows.

The linen was plain but crisp and white. Outside, the faint light from dim bulbs along the wharf made ghostly apparitions of the moored boats, ever at motion on the water. On the tables were small squat lamps, with low flames flickering in the chimneys. Time-worn window panes reflected the flames, like stationary fireflies, and haloed the light along spidery lines.

Two glasses were on the table, and the waiter brought a bottle of wine, for Nile to perform the ritual of tasting before he poured Nikki's glass. It was a homey place, unpretentious and intimate.

"To victory," Nile toasted, "yours and mine." As the glasses touched he said, "Here's to Demon Damon, the Queen of Hearts."

"Don't remind me about that article," Nikki said wryly. "I was so undone when I read it . . ." But what came after had driven it from Nikki's mind.

"You're not undone anymore?"

"No more than if you made good on your threat to tell everyone about Paris," Nikki said.

Nile gave a deprecating smile. "Isn't it the threat of Paris that brought you here?"

It was time she ended that particular charade. Nikki said, "You know I'm here because I want to be. Because I like you, Nile Bannerman."

On the surface Nile's face looked pleased, but for just a second something in his eyes recoiled. It happened so fast Nikki wasn't certain what she saw, but she felt as if she'd struck him.

There was a depth of feeling in Nile's voice when he said, "I like you, too, Nikki Damon."

Between them was an energy like the charge in the atmosphere before lightning strikes, sensory and silent, all but visible.

Nile broke the mood by saying something insouciant, and he kept the mood light as he ordered bouillabaisse.

"I hope your appetite is good," he told her. "This is fresh from the sea, and it's the best in Nice."

"My appetite is raging," she guaranteed.

Nikki delighted in the *baguettes*, long thin loaves of crusty bread that Nile would break, sending flaky crumbs to scatter on the snowy white cloth. Eventually Nikki's brimming bowl was empty. Nile poured the last of the wine.

THE DRIVE along the high corniche, having been spectacular in the last light of day, was terrifying in the dark. A narrow road clung to sheer rocky sides, but there was an overlook where Nile stopped the car and switched off the lights. In the distance was a breathtaking view of the city, lighted like a magic kingdom. They went to sit on the stone wall that edged the lookout.

The sea below seemed farther away than the canopy of stars above. Nile fitted Nikki against his chest, his arms surrounding her, and deep contentment flowed into her, coming, it seemed, directly from the strength of his embrace.

Scents of pine and wildflower softened and sweetened the tang of salt air. Faint night sounds accented the irregular crescendo of the surf. The cool moisture of the breeze played against the warmth of Nile's nearness. Nikki nestled into his shoulder and he pressed a kiss against her temple.

"I took a liberty on your behalf," he said.

"Umm?" Nikki replied, her response entirely to the vibration of his deep voice and the way it tripped her heart into a faster beat. She was sublimely unconcerned with anything he'd done on her behalf.

"I got Sybil to give you the morning off."

"Umm-mmm."

"I take it you don't object." He touched another kiss to that spot on her temple. Nikki brought her arms over his and lightly ran her fingertips across his wrists. He said, "It just so happens, I have the morning off, too." Nikki's fingers curled into his palm, and he pressed them closer. "We have so much to do—" His teasing, purring voice was indistinct. "Tonight we broke the bread, tasted the wine..." Nikki's breath caught. "That was a beginning. How long will it take to get to the end of your list?"

Nikki turned in the circle of his arms to give him her answer.

It was too brief a kiss, one they were both reluctant to end. "Nikki, this wall wasn't meant for people losing their sense of balance," Nile breathed huskily into her ear. "If I had to choose between you and the view...?"

Nikki nodded her agreement, and they abandoned the parapet. All during the drive back Nikki wondered if Nile felt as she did, hesitant and yet so eager, the freshness of a freely given kiss leaving her lips hungry for more.

Willingly she followed where he led her, back to his suite. Inside he quickly lighted the room, and Nikki expected him to embrace her just as quickly. Instead, Nile gave her such a thoroughly absorbing look that she finally asked, "Is something wrong?"

"Not at all," he answered. "I was just thinking."

"About what?" she said.

"Are you sure you want to know?"

"I don't often know what you're thinking," Nikki said softly.

"This is how you looked the first time I saw you." His low voice drew her closer. "I remember the color of your sweater, and the way you walked, how you wore your hair. The same way you're wearing it tonight."

Nile's lips met hers with such feeling Nikki was overwhelmed. He touched a wellspring deep within that flooded every fiber of her being, and sweet echoes of his name sounded in her heartbeat.

"Take down your hair," he said, but when Nikki reached to free it, he said, "No, let me." She had to help him with the unfamiliar pins. He carefully unwound her braids, slipping his fingers through her hair and drawing them down the silky length. "So beautiful," he said when it was free, burying his face in the mass of it.

Nile drew her down beside him on the sofa, and his lips found the hollow of her throat. Nikki's heart was wild inside her chest, and his ardor made her bold. She guided his hand beneath her sweater to the satin of her skin.

His lips touched her eyelids and grazed the line of her cheek, tantalizing until they reached her mouth, then seeking hungrily. "Nile..." Each kiss began and ended with his name.

She was shy of touching him. Her fingers twined in the inky darkness of his hair, thrilling to the texture of it. Yet at the wide-ribbed neckline of his sweater they were hesitant. Nile took her uncertain hands in his and brought them to the hem.

"Is this what you want?" he asked. Nikki nodded and he drew it over his head, flinging it aside in one fluid motion. "Here." Again he took her hands, and brought them flat against his chest.

Her touch against the fine sprinkling of hair on his chest sent shivers uncontrollably down Nikki's arms. A ripple of muscle betrayed Nile's reaction, and another followed as he drew her sweater from her shoulders a little.

Nikki's wide brown eyes focused on Nile's face, on sapphire eyes darkened almost to black, not daring to look at her hands, flowerlike as they lay upon his bare shoulders, which glowed copper in the lamplight.

"Beautiful girl," Nile murmured, and Nikki slipped her arms around him, pressing her cheek against the taut muscles of his chest. *Beautiful man*. His skin, warm and velvety, had an exotic scent of berry, and the pleasing traces air and sunlight always left. Nikki closed her eyes to revel in it, compliant as he slipped her arms from her sleeves and pulled her sweater over her head. "Lovely, lovely Nikki." She was anchored to his gaze, her fears calmed as he smoothed her disheveled hair and caressed her.

Nothing existed any more except his exquisite touch as he cupped her breast. Finally in urgency he sought her mouth.

What miracle created ecstasy like this? The kisses he gave her, took from her, were life itself. The universe could vanish, and it wouldn't matter. Nothing mattered except the man who set her heart on fire.

"Oh, Nikki, how I want you..." Nile murmured. Then his face was buried in her hair, his hands brushing it aside while he kissed the nape of her neck, and the murmur of his voice was strained. "More than I have ever wanted any woman."

"Nile—" Nikki turned away from him, half burying her head between her shoulder and his. "Don't say that—" She hid her stricken face, not knowing the tortured line of her bowed head spoke more eloquently than words.

"What would you have me say?" Nile asked. His jaw was clenched—Nikki could hear it in his voice. With rigid arms he held her upright, squarely facing him until she could no longer avoid his eyes. "Look at me," he commanded. "Don't turn away." His eyes wore the expression of one damned. "I can't tell you that I love you."

Nikki's reaction was stunned immobility. She couldn't bear to be only... wanted. Not when her desire for Nile was forged in the crucible of love.

What a terrible moment to discover it. Tears burned behind her eyes, enormous in a face gone pale, and she was powerless to stop them before they fell.

It was agony to look at Nile, his face etched with lines of anger, his whole bearing a recoil from an impossible demand she hadn't made. Deep distrust emanated from him, striking her in chilling waves.

What had she done? "Nile, I—"

His hands loosened the hold she'd been unaware of. "My mistake was in thinking you wanted me as much as I wanted you."

Nikki bowed her head, her hair falling in a curtain to shield her face. "I do...want you. But I can't..." She couldn't love him without telling him, and she couldn't tell him now.

"Here." He dropped his hands from her arms, reached for her sweater and thrust it at her. "I will not play games with you."

His rejection cut her to the quick. "Nile, please understand," she tried to say.

Nile took the sweater from her, bunching it and pulling it over her head. He was bitter in his look and bitter in his tone when he said, "I understand that what's honest isn't good enough for you. I've told you God's own truth. I wanted you. I still do." He sighed deeply. "But as far as I'm concerned there is no such thing as love, Nikki. I can't...make up fairy tales, and heaven help me, I don't want to hear them from you."

CHAPTER SEVEN

IF EVER TWO PEOPLE bore the bruises of rejection, Nile and Nikki did, but they were careful to ignore them. Instead they argued bitterly over inconsequential things. Injury hung palpable in the air, and they fought about whether he was to see her to her room. Anything to keep from touching those open wounds.

"You can't leave here alone, Nikki."

"I can, and I will. Don't come with me, don't talk to me, don't do anything!"

Nikki needed that outburst just to get away to the haven of her empty room. It hurt so much to be near him, to have him twist everything she felt into nothing more than games.

Without even changing into nightclothes she flung herself on the bed, boring her forehead into the pillow. "Why?" she moaned. *Why* to everything. Most of all, why to a heart she cursed for belonging to a man who didn't love her.

Sleep was an evil cloud that held her captive while the same scenes looped endlessly by. Nikki struggled to awaken, but the dreams played on. Nile's touch, the melting rapture of his kiss, and heaven, heaven in his arms until he rent her heart with, "I can't tell you that I love you. I can't make up fairy tales. I don't want to hear them from you."

The knocking at her door was insistent. Nikki got up, stiff from the position she'd maintained all night. Reluctantly she opened the door. "I'm not up—" she started to say, and then the words just wouldn't come. He was the last person in the world she'd expected to see.

"I know you're not," Nile said. "I wanted to find you before you got away. You were going to spend the morning with me."

Nikki protested, "That was before."

"Nikki." World-weary cynicism tinged his voice. "*Everything* was 'before.' Why didn't you just laugh it off at the very beginning? What did you expect, when you went on kissing me?"

Nikki had no answer, none that wouldn't meet with his derision. She'd been so badly mistaken in believing that what he felt for her was more than wanting.

"We'll have this understood," Nile said gruffly. "I won't go on kissing you. Things will be different from now on. Now that's said, you can get dressed."

"For what?"

"Contrary to what you seem to think, I *will* take no for an answer," Nile said. "What I won't do is let you back out on a day you promised me."

A quick shower was all Nikki had time for before hastily slipping on some walking shorts and a shirt and tying her hair back with a scarf. Maybe it wasn't wise to see him again so soon, when she was still so heart-sore, but when did wisdom ever steer the course of love?

Where he took her was an open-air market café in the old town, where the noise of the morning's commerce made her feel safe. They found a place squeezed against a row of boxed shrubbery and took the standard fare of coffee and a basket of croissants. They were surrounded by people, but there wasn't a soul Nikki knew. The bustle and the crowding had given them unexpected privacy.

Nile sat beside Nikki. He'd pushed the sleeves of his cotton boating sweater up, leaving his forearms bare, and his arm brushed hers. The contact was feather-light, but Nikki reacted instantly, jerking her arm away.

"Don't do that. Please." Nile took the hand she'd hastily withdrawn and brought it back to the table-top. Nikki's eyes misted at the sight of his hand dwarfing hers. "I don't want to be at arm's length from you, and I don't think you want that, either." The expression on her upturned face seemed confirmation enough for him. "Nikki, there is something I must ask you, and there's no delicate way I can do it, but after this I promise we will never speak of it again. Have you ever had a lover?"

Nikki's indrawn breath was audible, and her fingers stiffened under the warm blanket of Nile's palm. She turned her head away.

"You don't have to look at me, but I want you to answer. You've never had a lover, have you?"

"No."

The way Nile's fingers twined in hers must have been completely unconscious. "Then let me tell you something, as a friend," he said. "Don't go kissing strangers on the street. And don't ever, ever tell a man you want him unless you're sure."

Couldn't he tell how much she'd wanted him, how much she still did? Or what made her feel that way? "Oh Nile, you make me feel so horrible," Nikki said.

"You're not horrible," he answered, making *horrible* sound like a term of endearment. Then his voice turned bitter. "You just want a fairy-tale-perfect world."

"It doesn't have to be perfect," Nikki countered. Then softly, "And I don't want a fairy tale."

Disregarding her reply, Nile took her hand in both of his and turned it palm up. When he spoke, Nikki could tell he was trying to be truthful without being unkind. It wasn't possible. "Are you such a true believer that you don't know you've fallen for a myth? There is no place in my life for love, and I don't want there to be. I want what's real, or nothing at all." He looked at her hand and said, "If you ever have your eyes wide open, and you're sure of what you want, reach for it."

Nikki wasn't wounded by Nile's words. He didn't understand her, and she understood him only too well. She loved him, and he merely wanted her. She closed her empty palm and took her hand from his.

Nile gave her no time to sort it out, and Nikki was too shaken to do anything more than accept his assumption that they would still be friends. It was a crutch she could lean on.

She was shaky all morning, trying to pretend she could act the part. He was little better at it—so glum looking, it seemed to Nikki he was there because he said he would be, and she wondered why he wanted her company at all.

By late morning, he took her back to the hotel. The night owls were just straggling onto the terrace, some much the worse for wear. The Argentines, who'd apparently been out partying with Yvette, looked hung over. Nikki's team was matched against them today, and in a fit of gallows humor Nikki wished she could have a go at them now, instead of having to wait for afternoon.

Yvette came rushing onto the terrace, and she looked awful, a sickly cast to her skin and panic in her eyes. She spotted Nile and made a frantic dash for him. In the rapid, garbled burst of French, Nikki could only make out "It's gone."

"I warned you," Nile said sharply, scowling at Yvette. Then he was more solicitous, telling her to be calm, and steadying her with a consoling arm as he drew her aside. "Think, Yvette," he said. "Now tell me..."

It was strange to see Yvette's composure ruffled. Whatever could Nile have warned Yvette about? Curious, Nikki looked to see Yvette near to tears, as she leaned her forehead into Nile's shoulder. Nile gave her a reassuring hug and took her to a table, where he began to talk to her in earnest.

It wasn't so much that Nile left her without a word—it was the way Yvette had come running to him that gnawed its way into Nikki's mind. There had been the spat at the casino that had made Nile decidedly put out with Yvette, and something about her in a newspaper, something important enough for Nile to want his sister to look it up. Nikki'd had every intention of asking him about it, but yesterday she'd been so high on a cloud of happiness she'd forgotten. And today she thought of nothing but love newborn to the raw pain of rejection.

Nile had gotten up and was bringing Yvette with him. Yvette was much more subdued. With gestures that included Nikki, she said, "I am sorry to create a scene."

Nile was rather brusque in cutting her off. "It's all right, Yvette. We must hurry, now." Then, "Nikki, we're in an awful rush. Call my sister for me. Use the phone in my suite." He jotted the number on a scrap of paper. Then he fished in his pocket and handed her his room key. "Tell her to get copies of those articles and send them by courier on the afternoon plane." Over his shoulder he added, "Tell her to send a design drawing of Yvette's necklace, too." Pulling Yvette with him he strode away.

Inside Nile's suite the sense of his presence was so strong that Nikki almost made an immediate retreat. The echoes of tense emotion were still there, and it seemed she could hear their voices in the air.

Nikki found the telephone and dialed the front desk.

While she waited for the operator to complete the call, her glance strayed to the pile of notes beside Nile's chair. On top there was a single, folded page, and then writing on it began, "Break the bread and taste the wine."

"Mademoiselle Elaine."

Nikki hurriedly asked for Elaine Bannerman, and when she came on the line said, "Miss Bannerman, I'm calling from the bridge tournament, in Nice. My name is Nicole Damon."

"Oh!" The note in Elaine's voice could mean only one thing—those pictures were in *Paris-Match.*

Quickly, before she'd have to explain herself, Nikki said, "Nile asked me to call you. He wants a courier to bring some things on the afternoon plane."

"Ahh, he does?" Elaine sounded pleased.

"Yes. Some articles about the bridge tournament and pictures from the opera. And your design drawings for Yvette Broussard's diamond necklace."

"*Bon Dieu!* He was right." It wasn't pleasure now that Nikki was hearing. "Yes, yes, right away. What time is it now? Oh, I must go quickly—"

Elaine rang off in haste, sounding anxious and alarmed. It all came together for Nikki—Yvette's panic and the hectic rush to be away. Yvette's necklace was gone, and somehow, without being told, Elaine Bannerman knew it, seemed to have expected it.

Nile said he'd warned Yvette. How had he known? It was all so tangled up to Nikki. She asked herself a million questions and had answers to none of them.

She was about to leave the suite when she turned back and took her list from Nile's table. It wouldn't matter to him, but Nikki wouldn't want him to crumple it up and throw it away. For a while she merely stood there in the center of the room, her eyes squeezed tightly shut so she wouldn't see the words at the bottom of the page.

"I SHOULDN'T GLOAT over someone else's misfortune," Sybil said to Nikki, her eyes twinkling as she stole a sidelong glance at her opponents. "But the Argentines are dropping in their tracks. What happened to them?"

"Then went on a dinner cruise last night," said Nikki.

"Stay off that boat, then!"

"I don't think it was the boat—it was what came after."

"A bit of the grape?" Sybil asked.

"The whole vine."

Sybil chortled. "Let's go get them."

Nikki and Sybil came into the afternoon session with a commanding lead in the match. During a coffee break at midpoint, Sybil was certain the lead was growing. In spite of every promise Nikki made to herself not to do it, she looked for Nile. She saw him as he took a briefcase from a man who'd been waiting in the hall.

Nile spied her and came over to her. Nikki's hands were clenched, as if by holding on to nothing she could hold her heart in check.

"Would you mind a late dinner?" he asked her.

Somehow she'd had the notion he wouldn't want to see her again. "Are you still planning on that?" she blurted out.

Nile was quick to recognize the reason for her response. "Yes, I'm still planning on *that*. Nikki, nothing has changed except . . ." He gave her a penetrating look. "Nothing has changed."

A tournament director was calling the players back to the tables. Nile had just enough time to say, "Unless you intend to lock me out, you'd better hand over my key." When Nikki gave it to him, he said, "I have a lot to do after the match. It would save some time if you'd pick me up at nine."

NIKKI WONDERED if her judgment had deserted her. At any time in the evening hours she could have called or left a message for Nile and had her choice of ways to disappear. Even as she made her way to Nile's suite, she was telling herself to turn around. How was she to maintain the fiction of friendship, when the very sight of him made her heart ache for so much more?

At her knock Nile opened the door, and Nikki was taken aback to find Yvette there, seated on the sofa. Yvette was wearing one of her drop-dead ensembles, and she'd regained some of her self-possession, enough to give Nikki a quizzical and appraising look.

"Is it nine o'clock already?" Yvette asked.

Nile was putting some newspaper clippings into the briefcase Nikki had seen earlier. "I think we've finished," he said. Then, as if he'd just thought of it, "Nikki and I are going to dinner. Would you like to come with us?"

"I'm off to a show at ten. It should be diverting—they tell me it's rather naughty." Yvette was quite brisk, and it convinced Nikki she wasn't as eager to go as she pretended to be.

As soon as Yvette was out of earshot, Nikki said, "Her necklace was stolen, wasn't it?" At Nile's brief nod she asked, "What's going on? I talked to your sister and when I told her you wanted the design drawings, she said, 'Good God, he was right,' and hung up the phone. Has someone been threatening Yvette? Should you let her go off like that?"

"One at a time, please," said Nile, fending off her barrage of questions. "Let me get my jacket, and I'll tell you on the way. Our reservation won't hold past nine-thirty."

In the car he said, "It's a complicated story, Nikki, but I can assure you, Yvette's not being threatened."

Nikki broke in, "But you knew someone was after her necklace—I heard you say you'd warned her."

Nile geared the car down and headed deep into the old town. "I warned her because there's been a rash of thefts, from people whose names were in the paper, in those social write-ups where they tell what you were wearing and where it's from. You know the kind of thing I mean. Yvette couldn't resist showing off a little, and she thought she was doing Elaine a favor, getting her jewelry designs mentioned."

Nikki could easily see why Yvette would be featured in a write-up—she was a fashion photographer's dream.

Nile parked the car on a narrow street. He took Nikki's arm and in an unconscious motion let his hand stray past her wrist, and slipped his fingers through hers. No sooner had her palm touched his than Nile drew his hand away.

He offered no explanation, but his hand, now so impersonally at her elbow, was explanation enough. He'd resolved to treat her as a friend, and he was determined to do it. He led her through a doorway, up a flight of stairs and into a paneled dining room.

Nikki expected the maître d' to seat them at one of the candlelit tables, but he took them to a balcony overlooking the street. Flowers banked the railing, and crossed *flambeaux* lit the enclosure. For a minute Nikki was so busy taking in the way the torchlight reflected from an array of wineglasses on the table, she completely forgot how strictly she intended to govern her mind.

"This is so tiny," she said. "And so perfect." The balcony was completely private, on one side a curtained door and on the other, only the night. Deep rose-colored linen, flame sparkling from the crystal, the riot of blooms—the balcony was a small secluded paradise. A man didn't cloister a friend in paradise. That was meant for lovers.

Nikki held back a sigh. Nothing but pain could come from thoughts like those.

"This is the kind of place dreams are made of," she said, and her voice was a dead giveaway. She knew it when more than firelight flickered in Nile's eyes.

"This one is real," Nile said. The door opened and a waiter brought a bottle of wine. Nile tasted it and poured some into Nikki's glass.

"Go easy," Nikki said. "I don't want to wind up like my opponents today." The small enclosure was so much like a secret hideaway it made her voice whispery and soft.

"I will," he whispered back. There was a trace of the old Nile as he tilted his glass and said, "We'll only taste the wine."

One by one the courses came, *fruits de mer*, and a little salad, followed by lobster *fra diavolo*. With each, a taste of wine. "Notice," said Nile, "not a cream sauce among them."

Nikki laughed. "Do you make notes of everything people say?"

"I don't have to. Everything you say is memorable."

His manner said he meant it in jest, but Nikki's heart somersaulted just the same as if he'd been in earnest. "Why are you doing this?" she asked.

"Doing what?"

She swept a glance around the balcony. "Wining and dining me by torchlight."

"I'm testing my resolve," Nile said frankly.

Nikki raised a questioning brow.

"To see if I can keep from kissing you."

"Can you?" The minute she asked the question, Nikki knew it was a mistake. "Don't answer that," she said quickly.

"Then I'll ask you." All jest was gone.

"No, don't."

The night was so silent Nikki could hear the flames from the torches and the rush of air as she drew it into her lungs.

Nile said, "I'd think you were playing games if I couldn't see your face." His eyes narrowed, and his voice had a hint of that old cynical edge. "Does your face ever lie?"

Nikki shook her head slowly, but what she said was "I don't know."

She couldn't miss the irony when he said, "I ought to have better sense than to bring you to a fairy-tale-perfect place and ask such a damn fool question. This is a fine time to be turning noble, and why on earth I should do it, I don't know..." He sounded thoroughly put off with himself when he asked, "Nikki, what do you think of—uh—world politics?"

WITHIN A FEW DAYS Nikki knew what Nile was doing. By design he divided their time together into mornings off and evenings shared with mutual friends. Seldom were they alone, and even then he made certain other people were nearby.

At first Nikki expected him to gradually return her to her circle of friends, but his company remained constant. He could banter, but he didn't dance with her. He spent hours coaching her, but there were no more good-night kisses. He treated her like the best of friends, and it was obvious to Nikki that he wasn't going to test his resolve again.

It wasn't long before, inevitably, her team took its first defeat, and Nile was there to console her. "Did you really expect to beat Orsini? Aren't you the girl

who thought she didn't belong here in the first place?''
he asked her.

Nikki had been put into the match at the half, when
her team was already down by nine points. "We lost
by twelve," she said.

"Believe me, Emilio is walking the floor this very
minute, wondering why you're scared to death of him.
When he could only squeak three points out of you,
Nikki. He won't be calling you 'dear child' next time
you meet."

Nile's company was at once a torture and a delight.
If only she could, Nikki would take back those early
reckless kisses so she could have them now. *Now* when
they would mean so much.

Nile's friendship became the most treacherous gift
of all. With every passing day Nikki loved him more.

There was an afternoon when he was called away at
the break, and he returned with his eyes full of icy anger to tell her, "I have to fly to Paris right after the
match this afternoon. I'll be back in time to play my
half tomorrow."

He left her with no explanation and so abruptly that
she was still standing there dismayed when Yvette
Broussard brushed her arm. "The director's calling
you, Nikki." Yvette frowned a little as Nikki's eyes
kept following Nile's path. "You'll get a late play
penalty if you don't come along."

Nikki was disciplined enough to play the match
without letting her mind stray, but at the end of it she
still hoped for a glimpse of Nile. He must have left as
soon as the last card hit the table, though, and not
even waited for the scores.

Disappointed, she decided to spend the evening studying, but her room was so confining, she changed her mind and went to the dining room.

"We have a chair," Sybil called, waving her over to a table where she'd gathered an assortment of folk. Yvette was there, next to one of the Swedish team. "Where's Nile?" asked Sybil, before Nikki had taken her seat.

"He's gone to Paris overnight."

"I'm surprised he didn't take you with him."

Nikki's vague reply discouraged any more questions.

She picked at her food and wished she'd stayed upstairs.

The evening was interminable. Couldn't he have spared the time to tell her what was wrong?

Nikki fabricated an excuse to leave, and once away from the crowd, she kept on going, out through the lobby and across the promenade.

She dragged one of the mats close to the water's edge, where the waves would drown out all the other noises.

"Nikki?" Yvette's voice came like a phantom call, the one sound that didn't belong in the night. Her careful footsteps grated eerily on the loose pebbles, the only sign she wasn't a spirit materializing out of thin air. "Let me sit with you," Yvette said, and she settled beside Nikki on the mat. "I have watched you, not just this evening, and I saw the pictures in the paper..."

Nikki gave her a sharp look.

"In your country there is a saying," Yvette continued. "You are wearing your heart on your sleeve. Keep it there and you will get it broken."

CHAPTER EIGHT

NOT ON HER SLEEVE—in her chest, where the dart of
every word found its mark. Nikki eyed Yvette with
mistrust. So that was why she'd forsaken the bright
lights and come down to the beach. "Nile isn't trying
to break my heart," Nikki said as coolly as she could.

"You'll do it yourself," Yvette replied.

Nikki didn't want her hidden feelings probed this
way, and she tried to cut Yvette off, but Yvette
wouldn't be stopped.

"You think me cruel," she said, stalling Nikki's reply. "I don't mean to be. I like you, Nikki. You are
intelligent and sweet, but you are so artless and na-
ive."

Nikki felt she was being damned with praise.
"Yvette, stop it. You don't know what you're talking
about."

"Oh, but I do. I wouldn't have a minute's concern
for a sophisticated woman, but I am worried about
you. What do you know about the ways of the world?
Between you and the world there is no armor."

"I don't need armor," Nikki said.

"Don't you?" Yvette replied. "If you can say that,
you've proven you really don't know enough about
Nile Bannerman to keep from breaking your heart
over him. I will be blunt. You need armor against the
day you learn that Nile is never going to marry."

Everything Yvette said was like a dagger making random slashes and drawing blood. All Nikki wanted was for it to stop. Blindly defensive, she said, "You can't know that. No one can know a thing like that."

"He was engaged to the most suitable girl in France, and he walked out on her two days before the wedding. A man doesn't create a scandal like that unless marriage is poison to him."

Nikki was stunned. Had Nile abandoned one woman, only to find another, Nikki, conveniently nearby? It gave a new and sinister meaning to Nile's being "completely unencumbered." Yvette had found another vulnerable spot. Nikki said, "Have I walked into the aftermath of a scandal?"

"That was years ago," Yvette said, her effort at reassurance ringing false after the way she'd painted such a damaging portrait of Nile. "The scandal is in the past, and everyone knows he found a sensible solution. Now you must be sensible, too."

Sensible? If this was a game of wits, Nikki was overmatched and at a loss to deal with Yvette. "Why don't you just come out with it?" she asked wearily. "You have a reason for telling me all this. Do you want me out of the way? Are you his mistress?"

"Oh, poor Nikki," Yvette said, and she sounded genuinely distressed. "Have I blundered so badly? Nile has no serious liaisons. Even a mistress would be much too serious for him. Can't you see why you should guard your heart? If you must break it over him, then do it in secret, and let it happen later rather than sooner."

"Sooner?" Nikki echoed.

"He would put an end to this here and now, if he could see what I see. You are in love with him, and he is too decent to let that happen."

Nikki turned her eyes to the dark horizon and sat in stony silence. Yvette muttered a resigned "Ehh" and left her staring out to sea, trying to deny Yvette's deadly message.

She refused to believe it.

Yvette knew too much about the ways of the world and too little about Nile Bannerman. She hadn't felt the sweet, wild hunger in his kiss or heard what was in his voice when he said, "I don't need games."

Persistent phrases haunted Nikki's hopeful mind.

The shallow man Yvette described would have long ago turned to someone else. Nikki tried to fathom the mysteries of Nile's character. "He isn't shallow," she said aloud, to an indifferent sea. "If he was, I wouldn't love him."

NILE CAME BACK earlier in the morning than Nikki expected. He rang her room and asked, "What are you doing?"

"Laundry." Nikki was so happy to hear his voice, she practically sang her answer.

"I let you out of my sight overnight, and you go running straight to your detergent?" He sounded . . . wonderful.

Nikki laughed. "I couldn't wait.

"It figures. Why did I think that lilt in your voice was for me?" It was, and he knew it. "Can you tear yourself away? We still have a few hours before game time."

"Darn!" Nikki said. "Just when I was really having fun."

On her way down in the elevator, Nikki tried to decide if she would ask what had set him off in such a
rush to Paris. But he'd been so angry then, and his
mood was so different now—it seemed cruel to break
it. She opted to let him tell her in his own good time.

Nile met her beneath the stained-glass dome, and
even though his first words were nothing but a quick
rundown of their itinerary, it didn't matter. The look
on his face when he saw Nikki said more than enough.

Nikki cocked her head attentively as he spoke, but
the voice she heard was her own. *You're wrong,
Yvette,* she thought. Whatever was poison to him, she
knew it wasn't her.

A nuance in Nile's voice, a look on his face, were
little enough to build on, but they gave Nikki a fragile
confidence. Only a coward would let Yvette take that
away.

Nile had rented bicycles to ride around the town,
playing tour guide for Nikki, showing her all the many
sides of Nice.

"It's an old city of seafaring men…" The stories he
told her made it seem as though she could smell the
spices in the air. On one of the wooden boats there
might have been a dark-haired man who looked a little like a pirate.

To explain away her smile, Nikki said, "You're the
lazy person's guide to France."

Through a sun-drenched morning they rode around
the town, and Nikki was even less inclined to ask
about the trip to Paris. Nile didn't strike her as completely carefree, more as though he'd gotten things
under control—the way she felt when she knew a crucial project was going to come out right.

Near noon they found a fruit stand near the quay and filled a basket with dark, sweet cherries, bananas and nectarines. Seeking shade, they sat beneath a little tree and spread out a picnic.

"Who did you draw for competition today?" Nile asked.

"Mexico," Nikki answered. "How about you?" She bit into a nectarine.

"My compatriots, France Two."

Nikki's teeth clenched so hard she had to duck her chin into her hands to catch the fruit juice. The bottom seemed to drop out of her stomach. What if Yvette decided it was her duty to give Nile the benefit of her advice, too? The woman certainly wasn't derelict in her duty.

"Careful," Nile cautioned, handing her a handkerchief.

Tentatively Nikki said, "Will you be playing against Yvette?"

"I hope so."

Nikki gulped.

"I won't have the chance, though, if they're behind," Nile continued, and Nikki sent an urgent message to the heavens that Yvette's team would be behind.

Nile caught Nikki's eye. "Are you a little bit green-eyed? Don't be. Yvette will never be the bridge player you are. She's not serious-minded enough."

Memory came streaking to the surface at that phrase. "Is it a virtue to be serious-minded?" She wasn't certain she wanted to hear his answer when he didn't give one right away.

"Yes, it is." Even though he wasn't looking straight at her, she caught a twinkle in his eyes. "And it's a good thing you have such compensating virtue, considering you're ugly as sin.''

It had been ages since he'd said anything so outrageous, or since she'd laughed with him like that.

He offered her a handful of cherries, and Nikki ate them silently, savoring the way the sweetness burst on her tongue.

They walked onto the quay, wheeling the bicycles between them. Nikki ambled slowly, admiring the sleek lines of the moored yachts and reading the names aloud. "Ooh, listen to this one," she would say, charmed into dreams of faraway places. There were boats from everywhere. "*Reine de Corsica*," Nikki said, reading the name of one where a man bent over, working at the stern.

The man's head came up with an uneven jerk, yellow hair startling in the sun. "Oh, hello—Miss Damon, I believe?"

Nikki nodded. It was the fellow from the casino.

"And, Mr. Bannerman. Good day," he added smoothly.

Nile had stopped walking, and he leaned nonchalantly against the bicycle.

"We were just admiring your yacht," Nile said. "Is it for sale?"

Nikki found herself looking hard at Nile. She'd heard that tone before. He was fishing for something.

"Not this one," the man said. One side of his mouth gave a deprecating twist. "I can tell you're not a sailor, Mr. Bannerman. This is no yacht. It's just a pleasure boat."

"Oh, I see. Do you ever charter it?"

For an instant it appeared Paul Moray was debating his answer. Then he said, "On occasion, but I'm

here and there..." He looked as vague as his gestures. "There's so much to do. I don't make a practice of it."

Nikki wondered why Nile was prolonging the conversation. She decided to join in. "Such a lovely
name. Does it mean Queen of Corsica?" she asked
and was surprised when he gave her a look of calculating appraisal.

"Yes," he said, his eyes narrowed even more.
"*Queen of Corsica*." Swiftly he spoke again. "Were
you lucky at the tables?" he asked, and for a second
Nikki stared at him blankly. Then she realized he was
asking about her luck at the casino.

"Gambling's not my game," Nikki said evasively.
"I'd better stick to bridge."

Then Nile came to life. "Ah, yes. Wish us both luck
there, Mr. Moray. Eliminations begin in two days." A
moment later Nile checked the time and said, "We're
running late. But before we go, could you recom-
mend a place to eat?"

Nikki said, "We just—" and caught herself suddenly, finishing "—want a fast bite."

"In that case, go right around the corner at the end
of the quay," Paul Moray said.

Nile finished by inviting the man to lunch, but he
declined, indicating the work he had to do. She might
have been mistaken, but at that moment she thought
Paul Moray looked anxious to be rid of them.

Nile swung his bicycle around. "Stroke of luck
running into Mr. Moray, darling," he said offhandedly to Nikki. "Local people always know the best
restaurants." A little farther on he said quietly, "Put
your arm around my waist." Nikki did as he said and

felt Nile's arm slip around her shoulders. "Now look up and give me an adoring smile."

How long since she'd felt lost in eyes so blue they put the sea to shame? Not long enough to be immune to their power. Nikki didn't have to assume an adoring smile. It came unbidden, radiant on her lips and brilliant in her eyes.

The beginning of Nile's made-to-order smile began to disappear, but Nikki was still completely caught up in the spell of that magic moment, when Nile turned to look straight ahead.

His arm was still draped around her shoulder, lighter than a lover's touch, and making her dreadfully conscious of how firmly her embrace encircled his waist. He reinforced her doubts by slowly pulling his arm away, and Nikki, with a guilty start, swiftly dropped her arm and gripped her bicycle handle bars tightly, as if, by subduing the cycle, she could get a grip on her errant heart as it ran out of her control.

They were off the quay and walking faster when Nile steered her around a corner and stopped abruptly. His smile had vanished without a trace.

"Wait a minute. I want to see what he is doing. Hah! Get this."

Nikki peeked around, to see the *Reine de Corsica* pulling out from its mooring. Before it even properly cleared the traffic, it was racing into the harbor.

"Look at the speed he's making," said Nile. "That's no pleasure boat."

"How can you tell?" Nikki asked. "I thought you were no sailor."

Nile gave her a wicked grin. "That is what the man said, isn't it?" He propped his bicycle against a building wall and fumbled in his pockets. "Do you have any change?" As Nikki gave him all the coins she had, he continued. "While I make a phone call, order us some coffee at that little bistro. I'll only be a minute."

He looked full of purpose as his long strides carried him away. "Darling," Nikki repeated the word softly as she watched him go.

Nikki had coffee and bottled water waiting at an outdoor table when he returned. And questions. "Nile, stop keeping me in the dark," she said before he had a chance to sit down. "Why did you act so strangely back there? And what are these charades you're playing?"

"It's a long story, and I guess you have a right to know." Nile took a swallow of coffee. "Those thefts I told you about—"

"The people in the papers," Nikki said, to let him know she remembered.

"The thefts weren't random," Nile said. "They were all Elaine's designs. A couple of months ago someone broke into her shop, but nothing was taken. What he wanted wasn't in the store. A little later the thefts started happening, but I didn't see the pattern then."

Nile rapidly condensed the rest of it as Nikki tried to follow the twisting story.

"This came to my office yesterday." Nile put a note on the table, written on the kind of paper used for business memoranda. At the top was a logo, a green box with a white triangle in the middle, and a letter M. It said, "I too have a private collection now. My last offer stands." There was no signature.

Nikki pointed at the logo. "I've seen this," she said as her scalp tightened with apprehension. "Nile, do you know who you're dealing with?'' His expression said he didn't. "This is Mohsen Enterprises—tankers, shipping, oil. He bought Pacific Transport right out from under a friend of Sybil's, squeezed him to the point of ruin. This man gets what he goes after, and he doesn't care how. Nile, if his offer is halfway decent, sell him what he wants and be done with him.''

"No!" Nile said sharply, and just as sharply cut his glance away from Nikki. More softly this time, he said again, "No. I won't sell it." Nile's eyes were narrowed and intense. "But I will let his Mr. Moray think he has a chance to steal what his boss wants, and have him serve as bait to catch the bigger fish.''

"But if he tried to steal it once and failed, why should he try again?''

"Because this time it won't be locked in the vault. It'll be out where he can see it.''

"Not unless you sell.''

Nile said, "No one would fall for that ruse. But he might believe I'd given it away.''

"To whom?'' she asked then stopped short. "Oh... To 'darling.'''

"He knew your name, Nikki.'' When Moray had been in the casino she might as well have been invisible. "You're believable. No one else is.''

Her heart was in her throat, as she took in his earnest expression. "No one?'' she whispered.

"Nikki,'' Nile's voice was uneven, "I have no right to assume you'd do this. I've taken too much for granted.''

But Nikki was impatient to know what he had in mind.

The plan Nile outlined had been taking shape, she realized, even as he played out that charade with Paul Moray.

It sounded simple enough. Put the cause of all the trouble out in view. Nikki would wear a piece of jewelry and court the publicity she'd avoided before. Nile assured her she would always be surrounded by protective friends, while she acted as a tempting lure in a loaded trap. Nikki readily agreed.

"Don't if it's too unfair to you." Nile warned her. "I'm asking you to pretend to be...the Queen of Hearts."

Pretend. Of all the words he could have chosen, this one hit hardest. Nikki tore her eyes away from his. What could be important enough for him to ask her to pretend?

"If it will help, I'll do it," she said.

THE MORNING before the gala preceding eliminations, Nile went to meet the plane from Paris. Expecting another courier package, Nikki was astounded to see him return with a girl who could only be his sister.

Elaine had the same dark curls as Nile and a patrician face whose beauty looked serene until the wit flashed from purely Bannerman eyes.

"Nikki!" Nile beckoned her over and introduced her to his sister. At first, Nikki anticipated some awkward moments, but they never came. With Elaine she had instant rapport. In less than twenty minutes Nikki felt she'd known her forever.

"When does your match begin?" Elaine asked, and when Nikki told her, she said, "We have business to attend to," and promptly abandoned Nile. The "business" turned out to be an inspection of Nikki's wardrobe.

Elaine was all candor in her fashion commentary. "Elegant, sophisticated, but not for tonight." The black chiffon was cast aside. Fascinated by the reversible skirts, Elaine flipped them over again and again. "Clever," she called them.

"This is it." Elaine held the silver tissue blouse. "Rich but understated. It will be a perfect foil." Beaming, she turned to Nikki. "What style you have, Nicole. Your people must be French."

Nikki burst out laughing. In no time at all she was telling Elaine about her family, her career, her friendships, more than she'd ever told Nile.

Elaine said, "I hoped, no I expected you would be like this. You should have heard what Nile told me about you." Nikki could hear Nile's tone in the way Elaine quoted him. "She has a keen intelligence and courage. But she isn't quite sure she's ready for this level of competition. I think she could back a tiger down."

Nikki was wide-eyed, wondering if that was really how Nile saw her.

Elaine gave a shrug that despaired of ever understanding men as she added, "You look just like your picture. He didn't have to tell me how beautiful you are."

Nor would he. No man spoke of beauty unless he was in—

Nikki mustn't even think like that. Especially now. She mustn't speak of Nile at all. Elaine had a knack of inspiring confidences, and there was too much bottled up inside, too sensitive to reveal. Nikki made a rapid shift of subject.

"Elaine, just what is it I'm to wear tonight?"

"Nile hasn't told you?"

"Not exactly."

"Then I won't spoil his surprise."

Elaine sat at Nikki's elbow through part of the match, and when they met Nile at the coffee break she said, "I'm watching a winner. How are you doing against Yvette?"

Nile said, "They pulled her out after the morning round, but we're too far ahead for them to catch us."

Nikki breathed a sigh of relief. Nile hadn't played against Yvette.

"By the way, who won when you and Nikki played?" Elaine asked.

"The draw was random in the seeding rounds. We never played against each other," Nile said.

Elaine grinned broadly. "That's as it should be."

Nikki saw neither of them again until she was dressed for the evening. Her hair was loosely drawn into an old-fashioned style that Elaine suggested. Her throat and shoulders were bare where the curving neckline dipped. Nikki hadn't really noticed before how perfectly it was made to set off a precious jewel.

She was beginning to get a case of nerves. Cinderella to the ball, but with a twist. For Nikki there would be no prince.

Nikki wished they'd hurry, before she had too much time for second thoughts.

NILE CAME ALONE for Nikki. She opened the door to him, and as he stepped inside her room, the spark of his vitality rippled through the air.

It was all Nikki could do to keep from spreading her arms.

Nile went to Nikki's dresser and placed on it a rect-angular case covered in velvet and bearing the famil-iar golden *B*.

Nikki's fingertips caressed the letter's curve.

The tension in Nile's voice arrested her. "I haven't seen this since the day I locked it in the vault."

If he kept it locked away, it must be terribly valu-able. "Are you sure I can keep it safe?" Nikki asked.

"With me guarding it?" he answered. "You can safely give every one of the reporters a good look at it. Don't worry. No one will ever steal this from me." His harsh tone softened, and he said, "Go on, open it."

Her hands closed over the top of the case, meeting resistance when she tried to lift it. Nile's fingertips brushed hers.

"Push here," he said, and the case was open.

Nikki's hands dropped to her sides. "Dear God," she whispered. The jewel seemed to flame. It didn't look like stone at all. It couldn't be— It looked alive, as if it was fire meant to burn eternal in the heart.

How could a man own this and still believe there was no such thing as love? Nikki couldn't make her fingers reach for the necklace.

"Let me." Nile swept the jewel deftly from the case and stood behind Nikki as she faced the mirror. He brought the fire opal over her head, and she saw the back of the pendant, a strange design, intricately wrought in gold. Letters? Words? Yes, Nikki could just make out *"Mon coeur..."* my heart.

Nile bent to fasten the clasp behind her neck.

Did he know what he was doing, asking her to wear this? The rhythm of her breath quickened as the pendant settled on her breast, flashing scarlet with every beat of her heart. Nile straightened up behind her and met her eyes in the mirror.

CHAPTER NINE

NIKKI WAS ALONE with him again, and she hadn't expected to be. Not here in his suite.

The whirlwind evening had been a blur of faces, dances that had seen her passed from partner to partner, exclamations answered with, "From Nile," or "Elaine designed it" and "Yes, it's exquisite." Enough flashbulbs to make her think she'd been caught in a lightning storm.

It had ended with a little conference in Nile's suite where they'd all assured each other there wasn't a photographer in Nice who'd missed taking a picture of Nikki at the gala. Then Elaine had gone.

Now Nikki sat in a chair deliberately selected for its high arms and sense of confinement, with Nile across from her, equally confined, never taking his eyes from her face.

Every second that ticked by was one less chance that Nikki could ever break the bond of Nile's compelling gaze. Her pretence at his carefully constructed fiction of friendship had crumbled.

From the moment Nile had fastened that pendant around her throat, Nikki had known she could pretend no more. From Nile's hands the opal had fallen upon her breast and flamed with her every breath a signal that she was his. In the mirror, when Nile had lifted his head from fastening the clasp, he'd read it in her eyes.

The purest joy that had momentarily flooded his every feature swiftly disappeared. An instant reflex had frozen his hands atop her shoulders, then he'd averted his eyes and once more found iron control.

Throughout the evening those expressions had crossed his face again. He would look at her, and suddenly the light would kindle, and just as suddenly be gone—obliterated, as if there were a switch inside him, cutting off power at the first sign of danger.

Nikki got up from her chair, and Nile was on his feet. She ought to do something, but she was unable to move toward or away from him. "I should give this back to you," she said, reaching for the clasp behind her neck.

"Wait." Nile's hand, upraised, stopped the motion of Nikki's arms. His eyes, which had been constantly on her face, now dropped to the jewel. "Don't take it off," he said. The voice that could command now dropped to a hush as he said, "I don't want you to go."

Nikki's answer was a long time coming, but when she gave it she was sure. "I don't want to leave."

"Nikki, I..." Nile's voice deepened, hoarsening. "I have never stopped wanting you. But take care what you offer me, because tonight I am not going to refuse."

He told her to take care, and she did. "You haven't lied to me. I know it isn't the same for you," Nikki said. "It doesn't have to be. It's enough for me...that I love you."

Nile flinched from something so intense Nikki could almost imagine it searing him. "No, don't—" His breath was arrested in his lungs, but Nikki felt it as though she were the one struggling to breathe.

Then he was free of whatever had bound him and was driven into her arms. At first he seemed to resist the force of his passion even as he drew her near. Then his arms encircled her. He was breathing again, and with his breath came the whisper of her name.

In perfect stillness Nikki felt the pressure of his lips at her temples, on her eyelids. His kisses touched her shoulders, the hollow of her throat. Nikki understood that she was not to move, only to take from him in the gift of touch what he could not give in words. Nile's mouth found another hollow at her shoulder. He lifted her arms, caressing them and kissing her inner wrists, her palms, her fingertips.

"Oh, yes," Nikki said, and her arms were no longer empty. The depth of his longing showed in the tensing of delicate tissue beneath his eyes. His dark gaze sought her parted lips, and she lifted so that her mouth could be claimed at last.

Deep and sure, his kiss touched her as drops of rain touch the earth, bringing an end to thirst. He drew from her a rapture like the slow swelling of a far-off ocean wave.

How had she endured without his arms about her? How could she have lived and never held him again? What good was a life forever empty of his kiss?

Swift as the image was, it filled Nikki with a sense of piercing loss, just as Nile took his lips from hers. "No," Nikki moaned softly, and when he gave her teasing kisses, "yes, yes."

One hand cupped her face, and he pressed his cheek to hers. His whisper came urgently beside her ear. "Say it again."

"Yes."

He kissed her, too briefly.

"Nile . . ." It was an incantation, potent enough to bring his mouth to hers, hungry and demanding.

"Again."

"Yes." And then against the touch of his lips, "Yes, I do want you."

She unleashed in him such a flood of tenderness that she had no need to fear his passion. Her footsteps were sure as she followed him to the other room, her hands steady as she helped slip away her clothing.

She didn't begin to tremble until he loosed her hair and let it fall and buried his face in the scented silkiness of it, murmuring her name.

Nikki reached once more to unfasten the necklace.

"Leave it," Nile said. "I want to see it there."

It would be visible, Nikki thought, even if she took it off. Her eyes would see it branded there forever, the mark of love, her heart on fire. The opal flamed until it disappeared, crushed against Nile's chest.

NIKKI WOKE once but couldn't tell if it was night or day. "Where are your room keys?" Nile asked. "Sleep," he said when she told him, and she nestled down once more. It was bright daylight when she woke again to find Nile standing beside the bed, her bikini and beach wrap dangling from his hand.

"What's that for?" Nikki asked.

"For swimming, unless they're going formal at the beach these days."

It was the sight of his tanned bare legs and his muscular chest above his snug bathing suit that brought a blush to Nikki's cheek, not his reference to what she'd worn, and not worn, the night before.

Nile sat on the edge of the bed and pressed a cool hand against her burning face. He frowned. "Nikki, please, don't blush. Don't make me think you feel ashamed."

"I'm not ashamed about last night," she told him in a small voice. "I'm blushing because of what I'm thinking now."

"Now?"

Nikki loved it when his smile began in his eyes and slowly curved his mouth. She loved the glittering white of his teeth and the sheer joyous beauty of his face as it drew closer.

"I LOVE HIM!" Nikki sang every time she turned her face into the water. It came out only bubbles, and she swam more with abandon than with style, but it was the only way she could say the forbidden word. Today Nile swam much farther and faster than she did, and Nikki hoped it was because he felt the same as she. She felt alive, so much alive and so buoyant with the joy of it that she could almost fly.

He was more wonderful than anything she ever dreamed a man could be. In his arms she'd been created new. The woman who loved him yesterday was only a shadow of the woman who loved him today.

Love was a miracle. Nikki believed it, and if the miracle touched only her, it would have to be enough. She didn't understand how Nile could recoil from the very word, and yet in every other way be such a miracle himself.

Nikki swam until her muscles ached and then waited on the beach for Nile. Even miracles had to give way to the clock. They had to get ready for another day of competition.

By the time they got back to the hotel, the elimination flights were posted. The first team matchups were at the edges of the charts and a dwindling number of spaces progressed toward the center, where the winning teams would be filled in.

"We're not in the same flight," Nikki said. She'd looked for Nile's team and found it seeded first on the other side of the chart. She hadn't played against Nile in the seeding rounds, and unless she made it to the finals she never would.

"You did well," Nile said. "Look how high you're seeded."

"Right behind Orsini," Nikki said, "and in his flight." Her seeding would keep her from being in an early match with the Italian team. Her team stood a chance against the other teams. She wouldn't meet Orsini again until the semifinals.

The blank spaces on the chart looked threatening. They measured out the number of her days in competition. Semifinals—four days from now. Nikki traced the lines and spaces between Nile's team and hers, but in her mind his name was written on the final round while hers disappeared after the day she played Orsini. The blank spaces threatened her for another reason—they measured the time she knew she'd have with Nile.

IT WAS THE FIRST morning Nikki hadn't breakfasted with Nile, but she couldn't begrudge him the time spent in team meetings. Her team and his were entitled to their working hours. Besides, she couldn't expect him to neglect his sister while she was here.

Apparently he was neglecting her, though, for Nikki found no sight of him downstairs. Elaine had the morning papers spread out and invited Nikki to read them with her.

"Nile went to meet the police inspector," Elaine explained. "He won't be gone more than an hour or two." There was a splendid article about a match Nile played the day before, and Nikki was so caught up in reading about his play that she was slow to notice the pictures. The bridge columns were for serious stuff, but the social pages made much ado of "the lovely Nicole Damon, escorted as usual by an attentive Nile Bannerman, and wearing a stunning fire opal designed by none other than..."

"I hope that the thief reads the gossip columns," Nikki said. "They did everything but print a phone number for the charming Miss Elaine."

There was the inevitable Queen of Hearts picture, with the fire opal prominently displayed. This time the question mark after Queen of Hearts was replaced by an exclamation point. No doubt about it, the picture seemed to say.

Far more telling was the photograph that showed them together. Nikki remembered when it had been taken. She was pictured standing very close to Nile, and from the glow on her face it would take no imagination at all to decipher her feelings. It was much too late to regret having them on public display. She could only hope the intended message of that picture got to its target—that the opal was in Nice and would be here only as long as Nile Bannerman and Nicole Damon kept on winning.

Elaine said she wanted to go into the old town and wander through the *brocante*, a street market where all sorts of trash and treasures were on display. Nothing would do but that Nikki accompany her.

Among the market stalls they found the atmosphere common to bazaars the world over—charm in the jumble of oddments, melody in the haggling voices, curiosity in the search for treasure among the dross. Intriguing spice scent filled the air, and it wasn't hard for Nikki to imagine how it must have been when silks and spices, glass and pottery were hauled from wooden ships down to the local market, while oils and gold and precious jewels changed hands in quieter places.

She watched while Elaine bargained for a big straw hat, arguing and counteroffering as if a fabulous treasure were at stake. Finally a price was settled, and as an afterthought the vendor handed Elaine a bit of lagniappe as she counted out her francs. It was a keychain with a dangling plastic heart of a particularly hideous pearly blue.

"Isn't it ghastly?" Elaine giggled, when they'd moved a discreet distance away.

Nikki agreed. "Throw it away," she said.

"Oh, no," Elaine replied. "You keep it as a souvenir." She handed it to Nikki. "Maybe it's prophetic. A sign of our good luck with other hearts."

"Elaine, I never got to tell you how beautiful the fire opal is. It took my breath away. It was—there aren't any words that do it justice," Nikki said, speaking of that other heart.

"There never are," Elaine said quietly. "Everyone who sees it finds something different. It is enchanted, you know." Elaine went on as if Nikki's expression hadn't been so nakedly revealing. "You look at it and you see exactly what is in your heart." She looked at Nikki, hesitating as if she wanted to say something more.

Nikki tried to distract her. "On the back there was a design, but I couldn't get it all. I could just make out '*mon coeur*' and something else."

"Don't you understand French?"

"My reading's fair," Nikki told her. "I just didn't see all of it."

Elaine gave an odd little exclamation, then translated the phrase for Nikki. "It says, 'My heart is in your keeping.'"

There were words to do it justice after all.

"My heart is in your keeping." Nikki whispered the phrase to herself, her eyes threatening to brim with tears. For Nikki it was a truth so absolute, she longed to repeat it as a vow to Nile.

"Beautiful," Nikki said. "Nile told me it was your most important work. I can see why he can't bear to sell it."

Elaine smiled. "He turned down—I don't know the dollars—three times its worth."

Once more Nikki wondered how Nile could possess that priceless treasure and still believe there was no such thing as love.

"Don't you want to see it worn?" Nikki asked. "What would Nile do with it?"

Imps danced in Elaine's eyes. "What is he doing with it now?"

Nikki was about to say that he was dangling it before a thief, but her lowered lashes screened her eyes from Elaine's as she remembered how Nile had caressed her when she'd been clothed only in the opal.

NIKKI HAD A GLIMPSE of Nile almost as soon as she and Elaine returned to the hotel—just his profile and the line of his shoulder, but it brought fresh bloom to her cheeks. He hadn't yet caught sight of her. Yesterday, she'd have turned away rather than have him see her blush. Today, it was only words that were forbidden, and she didn't have to hide the look of love.

Before she quite reached his side, he turned as if he could sense her presence, and his eyes grew brighter when he saw her there. If not for Elaine, she'd have reached for his hand.

"Do you have news?" Nikki asked. "Elaine told me where you went."

"I do indeed," he announced, and in fact he was brimming with it. "The *Reine de Corsica* isn't registered to Paul Moray. Until eight weeks ago it was doing yeoman duty for Mohsen Enterprises of Kuwait. Moray's been mooring it here off and on. Now and then he tears off somewhere for a little while. Apparently he keeps to himself, carries no cargo and doesn't do anything else but keep the gas tank full."

"Nile! He's definitely tied to Mohsen, and we let him get away?"

"Not on your life. Although the police inspector I talked to says we have a chain of circumstance and little more. That note I was sent isn't even good evidence. He's not willing to go after someone so powerful without hard evidence."

This bit of wisdom met with Nikki's approval. In her opinion, there could be only one chance to apprehend the head of Mohsen Enterprises, and it had better succeed.

Nile enlisted Elaine's aid in preparing another stage of his publicity campaign. "Who'd have believed I'd be hatching a plot like this?" he said, as he directed Elaine to scout out a good location for a celebration dinner. Nile gave her the particulars of what he wanted, and she was to do the rest, he said. After some good-natured grumbling, Elaine was off.

Despite her fondness for Nile's sister, Nikki wasn't sorry to have her occupied elsewhere. Elated at the prospect of having Nile to herself, even for a little while, she walked beside him with a spring in her step across the promenade.

All the hours in the day wouldn't be enough to spend alone with Nile, and time was speeding by. Nikki longed for endless time, unbounded by clock or calendar, and most of all she longed to escape the ever-present crowds.

The beach was brightly lit by a climbing sun. Only a couple of hours remained before game time. They wandered along the shore.

"What are you thinking?" Nile asked.

"Oh . . . nothing," Nikki replied.

"Hmm. Have you been out in the sun?"

"Only at the market," she said. "Why?"

"I thought you looked a little pink, that's all." Sky-blue innocence, too good to be true, gleamed in Nile's eye. "Let me get a closer look." He lifted her face upward. "Yes, you are. What a lovely shade." The backs of his fingers brushed the curve of her cheek. "Aren't you going to tell me it's sunburn?"

"You know it's not."

The teasing look left his eyes. "It's hard to believe, in this day and age, there's still someone who can blush like that."

For half a minute he was silent, then he took her hand and walked quickly down the beach. Near the water's edge there were little boats to rent, and Nile helped Nikki into one. He rowed out past the few swimmers and shipped the oars.

"If you're careful," he said, "you can creep down to this end and sit by me." He took the cushions from the seats and used them for backrests, so they could lounge on the planking at the bottom of the boat. Nikki nestled into his outstretched arm. "How is that?" he asked. The waves rocked the boat gently, dipping the horizon in and out of view.

Nikki smiled. "Good. Almost perfect. From here it looks like we're in the middle of the ocean, sailing away." The heat of the sun came and went as a sea breeze played across her skin, making her drowsy.

He leaned his cheek against her hair. "This isn't at all like sailing," he said.

"It could be," Nikki said.

"Only in your imagination."

"A little imagination would do you some good. If you were sailing, if you could go anywhere in the world, where would it be?"

"Zanzibar," said Nile, sounding as if he were humoring her.

"Why Zanzibar?"

"It's an island. It starts with a Z. It must be at the end of the earth."

Nikki wondered if he ever wished he were that far away.

"All right," Nile said as if she'd asked him something, "we have an hour. I'll be very still and very quiet, and you can make up fairy tales about Zanzibar."

Nile slipped the edge of his hand underneath Nikki's and curled his little finger around hers, a simple joining that filled her with contentment.

A world away were duty and responsibility. Nile had stolen time, a small parcel of it for her. He nestled his knuckles into her palm, and Nikki smiled at the thought of her hand—too small to cover Nile's, yet in it his took shelter. Her fingers closed over the edge of his hand, and he locked them firmly there.

Nikki closed her eyes, and her thoughts were far from Zanzibar as she leaned into the rising and falling of Nile's chest as he breathed. When he spoke, even though his voice was low, the resonance of it became a part of her.

"On the other hand, an hour could be far too long. I'd much, much rather give you . . . a moment of my time."

CHAPTER TEN

ONE HOUR, drifting with the waves. For once Nile offered no excuse, no history lesson, no sight-seeing tour, no quizzes on bidding and play. He was simply there, doing absolutely nothing, and Nikki was simply there, doing nothing but loving him.

Blazing high and white, the sun climbed overhead, and as it slipped past zenith, Nile said reluctantly, "We have to go." He got onto his seat with an easy motion and steadied the boat while Nikki inched her way back.

Onshore he took her hand and held it until they went their separate ways.

In the shower she sang. As she dressed, she sang. Going into the tournament area, she was still singing under her breath.

Nikki was so in love it was effervescence in her veins, and it gave her eyes a luminous glow she thought no one else could see. It filled her with music no one else could hear. It amazed her that she could still do ordinary things, that when she walked her feet still touched the ground.

The hours away from Nile didn't drag. In those hours she earned the right to yet another day with him. Her team wasn't playing just for seeding anymore. One loss and the tournament would be over for them.

No one would have blamed Nikki if she'd broken under that kind of pressure.

In a match that was do-or-die, her opponents were rashly overconfident. One look at Nikki was enough to tell them the girl was head over heels in love. Some saw only the radiance in her eyes, and not the glow of purpose—and that was a mistake.

"I didn't have a minute's trepidation when we accepted an invitation to this victory party," Sybil told her later, an overstatement for which Nikki easily forgave her. Being the odds-on favorite to win their first elimination round didn't diminish the relief and jubilation they were feeling now that it was behind them.

These were the hours Nikki expected to drag. She'd won her guarantee of time with Nile, and now she wanted it, alone! The victory celebration was a dinner party for the two teams, and they were making it an all-out occasion.

In Sybil's presence Nile had told his reporter friend, "Nikki Damon's modest goal is to get by the first round of eliminations, and if she does it I'm giving her team a champagne toast."

Later, Sybil told Nikki the reporter had replied, "Are you kidding? *If* they get by? I've got money riding on her."

Elaine had put her time to good use. For the victory party she'd selected a restaurant where their table would be prominently on display.

Nile's choice of dinner partners puzzled Nikki. He was seated next to Sybil, leaving Nikki and Elaine side by side. She understood, though, when she saw how strategically he was situated. Their table was on a raised level, and Nile sat with his back to the decorative railing. Across from him Nikki was in full view of a crowded room. She could be seen by one and all, but no one could approach her without Nile knowing it. Without thinking, she reached for the necklace at her breast.

Word spread that the French and American teams were celebrating together, and there were plenty of interruptions by well-wishers. The town of Nice was gossipy enough, and the tournament interesting enough that a seemingly private dinner party was the center of attention.

The French players were treated as celebrities just as Nile had known they would be. Some of the visitors were perfect strangers, and this, Nikki realized, was the key to Nile's strategy. These people may not know bridge, but they knew the name Bannerman.

Nile made sure to emphasize his introductions of Elaine and Nikki, the designer and the wearer of the prize. People were as fascinated by Nikki as she had been of others that night at the casino, when she'd gotten her first glimpse of elegant gowns and jewels. Now the admiring glances came Nikki's way and turned wide-eyed at the sight of the flaming heart at her breast.

"All you have to do is be there," Nile had assured her when she'd voiced her doubt that she could cause a stir. "I promise you, the news will travel."

Nikki and Elaine had so much to talk about that the courses came and went, barely touched as they talked. Once in a while Nikki would meet Nile's eyes, find her pulse quickening, and in haste would look away. Even so, a fraction of a second was long enough for an unspoken message to arc like lightning between them.

The dinner ended at an hour early by French standards. After one champagne toast the waiters filled the glasses with sparkling water, the *sommelier* disapproving but agreeing that for tomorrow the wits must be sharp.

"How do you and Elaine find so much to talk about?" Nile asked when he and Nikki were alone again.

"We have lots of things in common. Mostly," she confessed, "we talked about you." Where to begin? Decidedly not with Elaine's whispered comment, "I wish my father could sit where I'm sitting and see the look on Nile's face now." Oh, the wild irrational hope that had sent Nikki's glance once more Nile's way.

There had been one not-so-personal revelation. "You didn't tell me you were the European champion," Nikki scolded.

"I'm surprised she told you that."

"I was looking for a little sympathy because we're in Orsini's flight, and she told me, if I wanted to worry about someone it ought to be you. Why didn't you tell me?"

"Would it have made a difference?"

"Probably I'd have fainted dead away," Nikki admitted, "and spent the rest of my time trying to hide from you."

"Which," said Nile, "isn't very different from what you did do at first." Nikki grinned another wry admission. "So the results were just the same."

He was joking, but even in jest he had it all wrong. "No, they weren't the same at all," she told him. "It's good you didn't tell me. I'm glad I didn't meet you with all your labels stuck on. You have too many." She would have been awed and overwhelmed, and she told him so. "It would have made too big a difference, Nile. This way I got to know the man."

For the longest time he merely looked at her, the merry twinkle in his eyes taking on a deeper, steadier glow, the blue growing darker and more intense as she watched his face. Nikki knew Nile could hear, as surely as if she'd said the words, "I got to know the man, and to love him."

Nikki half expected him to recoil, in one of those rending instants when he left her completely, responding wholly to something dark and secret deep inside. She found instead a man who searched her eyes, as if through them he could see beyond the dark.

She was in his arms without knowing how she got there, or caring—was alive to his every touch. Let him tell her if he dared, that love had no place in his life, that he didn't want it there.

IF NIKKI had to choose between loving and being loved, there was no choice at all. She would love. But she'd been wrong to tell Nile that it was enough. It would never be enough to be the only one who loved.

What had turned him into such a cynic? Nile could be so disdainful of his own happiness, it was like watching someone who refused to recognize the virtues in a foreign land. More and more, Nikki believed that to him, happiness was a foreign land.

On a day when they were going over study notes, Nikki idly glanced his way, to find an elusive expression on his face, and so clearly did it speak to her that she felt she was answering him when she said, "I love you."

He shook his head slowly. "Nikki, you know love is not what I want from you."

Why of all times it should come to mind now, Nikki didn't know, but she heard herself saying, "You must have wanted love once, or you would never have planned to marry.''

Nile's expression didn't change as much as it simply froze. ''Not every plan should be carried out.'' He sounded fatalistic.

''What changed your mind?'' Nikki persisted recklessly.

Nile said, ''It was better to put a quick end to it than to make a mockery of the marriage vows.''

Against his unassailable logic, Nikki had no argument. No man should take a vow he didn't intend to keep.

''You're right,'' she admitted. ''It is better than building your life on a foundation of lies.''

''Nikki, you want everything to be so damn beautiful. Take what's real. Honest desire is real, and you can put more trust in it than in all the other make-believe.''

Nikki looked at him steadily. Her trust wasn't in make-believe, it was in him, and what he was. She said, ''I promise I won't say it anymore.''

But he couldn't keep her from thinking about the maddening inconsistencies that flew in the face of his character. There were dozens of them, yet he was so consistent in other ways. There had to be a piece of the puzzle missing.

Another morning, out of a bright blue sky, a storm swept in. Clouds banked high over the sea, piling up until only a curtain of light fell sheer and golden at the darkest edge. Nile and Nikki were drenched before they could make a belated retreat. The skies were leaden, but for Nikki the day was lit by Nile himself. At times she would look at his face and find an expression that was achingly beautiful to see, and

Nikki would turn away, avoid his eyes, do anything to keep it there.

How could anyone not want that kind of happiness? Nikki cursed whatever had built the wall of distrust in Nile. Nothing could come near without running into that defense.

"Oh!" Nikki exclaimed aloud. "That's it. Defense."

"What about defense?"

"I just thought of something..." Something so important it was all she could do not to tell Nile. Nikki fumbled for a way to cover up her thoughts, and came up with an example of defending bridge hands.

"Well, I'm glad you're not wasting your time daydreaming. Do you want to go over some defenses?"

"Just let me think about it some more."

To Nikki insight was a killing gift, for it showed her what was missing. Not Nile's love, but his ability to set it free, name the force that often drove him headlong into her arms.

She had good reason now to keep her silence. As long as she didn't provoke Nile's defenses, love might have a fighting chance. Nikki was satisfied with those odds.

PLAYING THROUGH the elimination rounds proved not half the strain as waiting for someone to make an attempt on the fire opal. Nikki was sure one was afoot when she detected a strange man in the room next to hers, showing a lot of curiosity about her comings and goings. She told Nile about him.

"He's your watchdog," Nile said. "I've put everything into the hands of professionals."

Her feelings of anticipation increased when they went cycling along the quay again and found that, sure enough, Paul Moray had brought the *Reine de Corsica* back to Nice.

"Hello there," Nile called to him and stopped, as if to pass some time in idle chatter. Nile worked a reference into the conversation about how often they were out in the mornings and commented that he and Nikki were both competing. "If you're interested, the tournament's open to spectators." He gave Moray the starting times.

Underway again, Nikki said, "If that made any impression, I couldn't see it. We've got to do something to liven him up."

"Just keep dropping the crumbs," Nile assured her. "He'll pick up the trail."

The day before semifinals, Nikki spied Emilio Orsini on his way to his glittering missile of a sports car. She'd taken a close-up look at the chips of ruby red and gold in the paint and marveled at the way the sun made it flame, almost like the fire opal. It gave her the germ of an idea.

Impulsively she called out, "Mr. Orsini!" Would he do her a favor? He was "delighted of course," and half an hour later his car roared back into the parking lot. Nikki had a bottle of touch-up paint guaranteed to match the car. Orsini wondered what she intended doing with it.

"I'm going to try some magic," Nikki told him.

Orsini chuckled. "You think by tomorrow to put a hex on me?"

"On someone, Mr. Orsini. But it'd take more than a hex to deal with you." And a win today to have the chance. "Thanks again for your help."

Nikki bought a bottle of nail polish from the gift shop and a flimsy gilt chain and hurried to her room with both. She pried the hideous blue plastic heart off its key ring and hung it from the chain. Then with the nail polish brush she stroked the touch-up enamel on it until the blue heart was covered with the same glittering flash as Orsini's car.

"There," Nikki said, satisfied. Just wait till she told Nile her idea. The bauble was a little larger than the opal, and up close it looked exactly like the piece of junk it was. But from across the room... Maybe it would do, if it was what the eye expected to see. Nikki hung it to dry in her closet.

She was only a little late in meeting Nile. He'd reserved a tennis court for them, and she'd cut the time too finely.

"Let me guess," he pretended to ponder, "laundry again?"

"Nooo," she said, teasing.

"You couldn't have been out with Elaine. She can't do anything in under an hour."

"I wasn't out, I was in," Nikki said. "That's all I'm telling. It's a surprise."

Nikki's strictly recreational tennis game was no match for Nile's far greater skill, but she fought hard for the points she scored.

"You never give up, do you?" Nile asked her.

"Hardly ever," Nikki said. She was panting from her effort and wringing wet and exhilarated. "Now that you've trounced me, you can confess, if you happen to be the European tennis champion."

"Not by a long shot," Nile said. "I just like sports."

"You certainly don't go at them halfway," said Nikki.

"Why go at anything halfway?"

Nikki smiled to herself as she toweled off. "My sentiments exactly," she said.

"Nile, before I get cleaned up you have to come with me. The surprise should be about ready."

At the hotel she marched him to her room and rummaged into the closet, pulling out the counterfeit necklace on its hanger.

"Where in blazes did you get that?" Nile said. Then, looking closer, "What is it?"

"It's just a plastic key chain, but it fooled you for a minute, didn't it?" She let Nile get a really close look. "This is Italian fire-bomb red. Mr. Orsini got me some paint to match his car."

"What are you planning to do with it?" Nile asked.

"Use it for bait," she answered. "You want to catch a thief, but how can anyone steal the opal? When I'm not wearing it, it's locked in the hotel safe. Time's running out, Nile, and your man hasn't made a move. With a decoy you can push him a little, take a few chances. Let me wear this out, alone—put it close enough for him to grab it."

"Absolutely not!" Nile's voice thundered. "He's supposed to steal it *from* you, not *off* you. This is for professionals to handle."

"Professionals have been handling it, and nothing is happening," Nikki said.

The set of Nile's face was argumentative. "Something will happen. I'm sure of it. Now throw that thing away, and don't get any more of these ideas."

After Nile had gone to get ready for the afternoon's competition, Nikki wondered if he felt the pressure of time the way she did. He called his office daily but never spoke of going home. For that matter neither did she, but she thought about it and dreaded the day. Nile couldn't just let it end, could he?

Nikki went against stiff competition for four grueling hours. The scores were inching back and forth. At no time was she certain of a win. The match came down to the last hand.

Pleasure blended with weariness as Nikki became aware of the crowd. She was always a little surprised that so many people materialized the instant the competition ceased. She looked for Nile and, seeing him across the room, felt revived. But she lost him once more in the general melee of scoring and didn't find him again until the crowd thinned out.

Nile, usually so willing to give interviews to the working press, whisked Nikki out of the room before any of the reporters could corner her. "Let someone else do the honors. I want tonight to be just you and me."

THE NIGHT had a fragrance of its own. Nikki leaned back against the roadster's seat and tried to identify the scent as Nile drove. Thousands of flowers perfumed the way, and as the road went winding higher, pines and the leafy tree scent stole into the air. The short drive was a trip into another world. Nikki was glad she'd seen Nice the way Nile showed it to her, and she told him so.

"There's so much more I'd have liked to show you. I should have taken you to sail in the harbor," he said. "There's never enough time...."

Time. He did think of it after all.

Tonight she wanted that timeless feeling, visions of an endless procession of hazily beautiful days, lazy and slow, bathed in a rosy glow.

This was all she wanted—to fill her senses with him. To see infinity in the dark depth of his eyes. To hear the sound of his voice so near it echoed in the drumbeat of her heart.

"Oh, Nile, I—" Words so faintly spoken they were more felt than heard, words that spilled from her lips before she could stop them.

CHAPTER ELEVEN

TRY AS SHE DID to fight it off, Nikki wasn't able to keep time at bay. It was daylight. Execution day. She was to play Orsini.

Before she could turn her face back into the pillow and try to recapture the feeling of having infinite time to be with Nile, her alarm sounded.

Stifling a groan, she got up quickly and rushed to shower and dress. Nile would be waiting for her.

"Wouldn't a walk be as good as a swim?" Nile asked, when she came up to him at last, her eyes shining. There was a boat idling back and forth, close to where they usually swam each morning. "There's too much traffic out there."

"It's only one boat," Nikki said, but it showed no sign of going away, so she agreed to the walk instead. Nile took off so briskly Nikki couldn't keep up without breaking into a jog. "Slow down a little—your legs are longer than mine."

He did but not without ribbing her. "Sybil wouldn't let you get away with this."

"She knows I'm not the sluggard in the crowd." At a more comfortable pace it was easier to talk. "Besides," Nikki told him, "she says I'm getting sharper every day, thanks to you."

What Sybil actually had said was, "If this is what moonlight and love songs do for your bridge game, I ought to be sponsoring Nile Bannerman myself."

"Sharper every day, hmm? In that case, you ought to be optimistic about your chances today."

"That's different, Nile. Emilio Orsini was a champion when I was still in pigtails. He's a legend."

Nile said, "That he is, Nikki, but all you owe him is respect. Let him remember you as a worthy opponent, not a pushover."

They got back to the terrace with time to spare before team meetings. The table Nikki thought of as hers was occupied, and she felt a small tug of regret before they settled for another. She gave the crowd a sweeping glance. Nile was behind her, pulling out her chair. "It's so strange with only four teams left," she said.

"You didn't think it would go on forever, did you?" Nile asked. Nikki's heart gave a lurch, but Nile only slid the chair beneath her and walked around to the other side of the table, continuing as if it were all one train of thought, "With half the field eliminated each day, it doesn't take long to thin out the players."

She must be even more nervous about today's match than she thought, the way she was reading hidden meanings into everything Nile said. Her mind was playing tricks, to make her hear ominous hints in every innocent remark he made.

Team meetings cut into the morning, and this time there wouldn't be an hour or two when she and Nile could disappear. In a match this important, the strongest pairs played all the way through.

"Let me start early, Sybil." Nikki was restless to get into the contest. Without Nile the hours loomed empty, and idleness wouldn't make them go any faster. "Let me play all day."

"You want to anchor the team? Today?"

"I'm ready," she said to Sybil. "I'll never be more ready. Thank goodness we've got the open room." Nikki's aversion to playing in a closed room was well known.

"On one condition..." Sybil started to say. Then she smiled. "Full speed ahead, Nikki."

For the semifinal round only two tables were set up in the large room, but it seemed more crowded than the day the tournament had begun. Spectators circled the tables four rows deep.

Nile was at the table in the center of the other circle, and Nikki signaled to him. Once she was seated she could no longer see him, but knowing he was there gave her spirits a lift.

The tournament director was announcing the seating of the players in the closed room upstairs. When he announced Orsini's position, there was a buzz of sound around the table. Nikki was in the identical position of play as Orsini. And when the duplicate hands were given out upstairs and down to begin play, she and Orsini would hold the same cards.

She could almost hear Nile's voice reassuring her, saying, "Don't you realize you have an advantage?" Orsini was the most analyzed player in the history of bridge. He'd practically written the texts, and Nile had used them to tutor her, boosting her morale with, "You're taking a course in how he thinks."

"That's it!" Nikki exclaimed.

"What? Don't tell me you *like* sitting in Orsini's chair."

"Sybil, Nile has seen to it that I've done my homework." With Nile unavailable, Sybil was the recipient of Nikki's thankful smile. "We've got him just where we want him."

"And I thought I'd heard everything," Sybil said, nodding her head. "I have to hand it to you, Nikki, you really do have nerves of steel."

Two hours later there was a short break. Now was the time Nikki felt sorry for the players in the closed room. They were confined for the duration of the match. At least she could take a little walk.

Nikki spied Nile and Elaine talking in the hall. Nile thrust a square brown envelope into Elaine's hand, and a second later she scurried away.

"Hello!" Nikki called, and it seemed to her that Nile was startled to hear her voice. When he turned around, he wore a smile that looked uncomfortable, like something he'd put on in haste, and it didn't quite fit. "How's it going?" she asked.

"They're tough," Nile replied absently, "but I think we'll get them."

"I don't doubt it," Nikki said. He was hiding something, she was certain of it. Maybe his team was down, and he didn't want her to worry. But that was so unlike him.

"No nerves?" Nile asked after a moment.

"No. After your pep talks I was feeling fierce."

"And are you still fierce?"

Nikki smiled up at Nile. "I'm respecting the daylights out of him. Before I make a bid or play a card, I ask myself 'What would Orsini do?' and then I do it."

Nile's lopsided grin was spontaneous. "Then you're not scared of him anymore."

"I'm scared out of my wits, but I'm not playing on my wits. I've borrowed his."

A minute more, and the game was underway again. Another two hours, and the first half was over. One minute Nikki was all adrenaline and the next, in limbo. She said a quiet prayer. "Please keep us in this match. Let me go the distance."

"Well, well, well!" Sybil thumped the scorecard. "I believe we've done a morning's work."

Nikki found Nile standing with Elaine in the glass-walled hall by the terrace. "We're up by one!" she told him.

"One is enough." He took both her hands in his. "For that you deserve a medal. Now if you can just get by Orsini this afternoon."

"I thought you said he was nothing to worry about."

"Oh *worry* is another matter. If you hang on this afternoon you can start chewing your nails about tomorrow. Beat Orsini today and I'll give you a medal. Beat me tomorrow and I'll give you the opal."

Absolute shock hit Elaine's face, her eyes startled and as round as her open mouth. You'd think she believed Nile actually meant it.

"I'll take that as an indication of how much chance you think I have," Nikki remarked.

A small buffet lunch was almost ready on the terrace. Nikki excused herself, promising to join Nile and Elaine soon, and went up to her room. Her only purpose was to indulge in a little whoop of victory, dance a little undignified jig to let out some of her excitement, and just plain wallow in the thrill of leading at the half.

Nikki opened the closet to take out a fresh blouse, and her hand bumped against the painted plastic heart. In her present giddy state she couldn't resist taking it out and waving her fingers in a spell-casting pantomime. "Abracadabra shaboom, we've got you now!" She could share the joke with Elaine and Nile later. They would appreciate the idea of putting a hex on Orsini. Nikki popped the heart into her purse and hurried back downstairs.

Outside, the sun was blinding bright, and the terrace looked hot. Nikki could feel the heat through the glass wall, in the spaces that weren't shaded by tall potted plants. Nile was seated near an open door, his back to her, and he was deep in conversation with Elaine.

Nikki paused and edged closer to the door, to have one surreptitious peek at him. The breadth of his shoulders, the handsome way he carried his head, the riot of dark curls that would soon need cutting.

Elaine looked worried about something—it showed in her face. "You can't!" Nikki heard her cry, and she watched as Nile leaned across the table so far that his jacket strained at his shoulders.

What Nile was saying at first was too low to be heard, and then the urgency of the situation made his voice angry sounding and penetrating.

"No need to worry. That opal will never belong to some glorified mistress."

SCALDING TEARS brimmed in Nikki's eyes, but they wouldn't fall. Mistress! He didn't even give her that much. "Glorified mistress" was what he called her. Nikki was so humiliated she could only cringe into the shadow of the greenery and let the pain sting across her face. She wanted the earth to open up and swallow her. She was shriveling up inside, but she couldn't make herself small enough to disappear. She shrank back from the window wall and hugged the other side of the hall as she fled.

She bumped through the door to her room and locked it behind her, then panicked at the sound of her own rasping breath. Her cheeks were wet, and she didn't know when the tears had come.

Strangling on a sound that lodged in her throat, Nikki fled into a shower where torrents of water washed away her tears, but nothing could drown out the sound of the telephone as it rang and rang and rang.

Later, with damp hair braided, Nikki appeared at the door of the Considine suite, composed and under control. No one looked too closely at her eyes.

Sybil said, "Nile rang up. He said to call if you came by."

"I found him already," Nikki replied noncommittally.

The hubbub resumed, with everyone in the room talking at once. But Sybil just gaped at Nikki. What the men couldn't see Sybil could. "Come here," she said to Nikki and led her into the other room, away from the jibes about Nikki's newfound thirst for blood. "Talk," she ordered.

Briefly Nikki told her. Not everything, but enough.

"Nicole, that man is so in love with you," Sybil argued, "you're blind if you don't see it."

Bitterly Nikki denied it. "No. You don't know what *that man* said about me."

"And you won't tell me."

Nikki shuddered. "I can't. I'd rather play," she said, then realized how much she meant it. She would fall apart if she were left alone.

Sybil said finally, with a resigned sigh, "I should pull you, but all right, Nikki, you've got your game. Let's go."

There was one condition. "We'd bloody well better win this match."

"I didn't come here to lose," Nikki said.

EMILIO ORSINI wrung every drop of drama from the situation. Nikki would play where he chose, against whom he chose.

"Miss Damon and Mrs. Considine will play in the closed room."

They were cut off from the world, playing in a closed room. It always felt like being thrown into a pit. This time, though, Nikki didn't have that awful isolated feeling. She wasn't locked in—Nile Bannerman was locked out.

"You may begin." The match was under way.

If the early half had been a sharp cool mental struggle, the second had all the heat of a physical battle.

Hour after hour the fires of Nikki's private hell burned white-hot, creating an energy so destructive that using it against Orsini was pure relief.

She put her worth on the line against him for four more hours. Let him be the measure of what she was made of.

"That was the last hand, Nikki." Nikki had to hear it twice before it sank in. She had to be urged out of the suite and into the elevator, down to the large room where the first person she saw was Nile Bannerman with his loving, lying eyes.

The crowd swallowed him up. Across the room there was a roar, nearly drowning out the announcement that the Bannerman team had made it to the championship round. Nikki forced her attention to her own scorecard, where a steady progression of numbers mounted up.

"On your feet, Nikki. They're coming over," Sybil ordered.

Never face the team you've beaten sitting down.

Nikki's face was burning, but her teeth were chattering, and her hands were like ice.

Orsini took her hand. "I hope you win it all," he said and tried to rub some warmth into her icy fingers. His tired eyes saw too much. "You played your heart out, my gallant little friend." Then he smiled and looked beyond her and was gone.

The crowd surged forward to congratulate the team, and then they too were gone, the last of them commenting, "She still can't believe it."

"Oh, but *I* can," Nile's deep baritone struck a vibrant chord even though Nikki tensed every muscle when his hand touched her shoulder. Her mind rejected, while her heart rejoiced and went on rejoicing in spite of everything she did to stop it.

Her teeth were clenched so hard her jaw ached, and her eyes burned bright and dry. Nikki evaded him, wouldn't look him in the eye. So reluctant was she to talk to Nile that he finally led her, protesting, to the farthest corner of the room.

"You're about to jump out of your skin. Let's go somewhere and relax."

"No! I . . ."

"Nikki." Nile took her cold and trembling hands, looking at them in dismay. "You've worn yourself completely out." The harder Nikki tried to avoid looking at Nile, the more deeply he searched her face. Lying eyes, lying mouth, lying voice that melted low into the sweetest murmur. "It will never be this bad again."

Wouldn't it? When would her heart stop flaying itself against the cage her mind was trying to build around it? It would always be this bad, unless one day she could break the habit of loving him.

"I suppose not," Nikki said, more of a liar than he.

Nile brushed the backs of his fingers across her cheek. More than anything Nikki wanted him to warm her hands with his, turn back the clock and make it yesterday. Give her back the sheer blind foolish trust that had made her believe it was so right to love him. Dear God, she *still* loved him!

Nikki turned her face away. Stonily she said, "Let me go, Nile. There's nothing left. Everything is all used up."

Nile's hand still lingered at her cheek. "Nikki, I wish..." his voice caught, imitation emotion that sounded so sincere. Yesterday she'd believed it was real. "I couldn't hold you in my arms tonight and compete against you tomorrow."

Here was escape, a chance to run away, but Nikki's feet wouldn't move. "You couldn't..." she repeated.

"You shouldn't have used everything up against Orsini. Get some rest, Nikki. You look ready to drop."

So that was how a superficial relationship ended. Yvette Broussard's warning came back to haunt Nikki, another terrible truth she hadn't wanted to see. She really did need armor, and she hadn't any.

What an arrogant fool she'd been to believe her eyes saw more clearly than anyone else's. Twice a fool to dream impossible golden words were meant for her, when they were only what she wanted in her heart to hear. Three times a fool to catch herself almost believing once again all the unsaid things.

Nikki's room was no refuge at all. The telephone rang immediately, and if she could have endured the sound, she wouldn't have answered it.

Sybil was calling. "Are you coming with us? We'll wait for you."

"No, I just need to be by myself for a while," Nikki said. The thought of facing anyone, even friends, made her sick. "Go without me."

Sybil took her most authoritative tone. "You're not as calm as you sound, Nikki. Go to my suite and order up from room service. Watch television. Stay the night, if you need company later. This isn't over yet."

Grateful to look at walls other than her own, Nikki did as she was told. She even tried the television, but it didn't help. She curled into a corner of the sofa and picked up Sybil's notes.

"France Premier," she read. "Maison Bannerman."

CHAPTER TWELVE

NIKKI DIDN'T LIKE what she saw in the mirror. That girl was wounded, pale, with a faintly bruised look beneath her eyes.

Sybil saw it. "Do you want to sleep in this morning?"

"No, I want to get it over with."

"Haven't you talked to him? Can't you straighten it out?"

"No! He's said everything there is to say."

"I suppose you know best." Sybil sighed. "I'll do what I can for you, Nikki. I'll ask for choice of opponents instead of seating. We can keep you away from his table."

"Don't ask them any favors, Sybil. I don't care where he plays."

Sybil said kindly, "You've always been strong, Nikki."

"I know I'm strong," Nikki replied. "Now I want to learn to be tough. I want to be armor-plated."

Before the competition began, Nikki wouldn't let Nile catch her alone. "I called you this morning," he said accusingly, trying to get her away from the crowd.

"I wasn't there." She kept moving.

"Nikki—"

In spite of everything, Nile could speak her name in a certain way, and in her secret self there was an answer. When Nikki took her place at the bridge table, she was shaking.

Those hours spent studying Orsini would have been better spent studying Nile Bannerman. How good he was became evident on the first deal.

Nikki got off to a faltering start. Now was when she needed that inner fury that gave her the will to fight, but it was gone, burned to a dead cold cinder the night before.

Her play was erratic and unpredictable, costing points where the scores should have been equal.

At the break Nile confronted her even before Sybil had a chance. "What has happened to you? You ought to be flying high after yesterday." He stopped her from replying. "Go take a walk, get yourself together, and when you come back I want to see Nikki the Demon Damon. Do you understand me? I want the best that's in you, Nikki. Now give it to me."

If he was trying to shock her, he succeeded. Until now Nikki had felt so hurt she'd spent her strength fighting the wrong man. Orsini's respect she already had. It was time to wrest some respect away from Nile Bannerman.

Nikki walked back into the playing area. Chin up, shoulders squared, she looked Nile straight in the eye, and his face became sunlight after rain. *Smile all you want to,* Nikki thought. If she died trying, he'd remember her as a worthy competitor. This one was for her pride.

The rest of the morning session came down to the final deal. Nikki thought of the points she'd lost. To win them back, she'd have to get them now.

She studied the play. There were two losers, and she could only afford one. Nikki could save the contract if she could kill Nile's diamonds with her heart trumps, and keep the last one as a winner. This had to work.

"Small diamond." At last Nikki called the card to lead the crucial play and was prepared to play her remaining high trump. The slam was so thin it took desperation to bid it—but it was coming in!

A card lay on the table in front of Nile, and for the space of a long deep sigh Nikki stared at it—the king of diamonds, fallen like a surrendered battle standard.

Nikki won the hand with the queen of hearts.

No KID-GLOVE treatment for Nikki anymore. "You butchered three easy hands!" came from a teammate, and from Sybil, "More than three, but they didn't believe she could be that awful and misplayed themselves into minus scores." Groans. "But you got it back on the slam." No one could resist telling Nikki that the slam she bid was insane.

"A tie." Sybil took the score sheet to verify. Then she muttered, "It's out of our hands now, and I for one will be glad when it's over. We made it to the championship round, and we can leave it with our heads up, no matter what happens now." She made a fist and gave Nikki's chin a playful brush with her knuckles. "Come on, Niks, I'll buy you some lunch."

"I think I'll get some air instead," Nikki said, bent on getting away before Nile found her. Slinging her purse over her shoulder, she was out of the room before any of the curious onlookers could approach her.

Dumb luck, that's all that had saved the morning. Nikki had made too many errors and paid too small a price. The French team had tried to find logic in her early irrational play and been punished for it.

Even Nikki's redeeming slam had been unde-served, an Orsini-like grandstand play. If she'd been in her right mind, Nile's team would have beaten hers. Nikki had no doubt about it.

Gritty sounds came from Nikki's soles. She was in the parking lot. Lord, she was weary of this place, and she needed somewhere to go and lick her wounds. Maybe a walk to the beach would soothe her.

"Keep going straight ahead, Miss Damon." It was a monotone rasp of a voice. Then she saw sunlight on neon-yellow hair, pale unblinking eyes, as Paul Moray said, "I've been sent to bring you to luncheon."

Nikki went momentarily blank, unable to act, and that gave the man at her side the advantage. He pro-pelled her a few feet and pushed her into a strange dark car, before walking around to the driver's side. Nikki promptly grabbed the door handle.

"Don't" came a voice from the rear seat, and a hand was thrust forward to restrain her.

There were two of them and only one of her. Nikki wasn't brave enough or fool enough to try to get away.

Moray drove to the dock where the *Reine de Corsica* was moored. Escape from the car might be im-possible, but there was no way the two men were going to get Nikki off that quay and onto the boat without a struggle. The minute she was out of the car she broke away from one, but Moray, deceptively quick, jerked her to a stop.

"Help—" Nikki started to shout but was cut off by Moray's hand clamping over her mouth.

"Miss Damon," he said in a put-out tone, "you are not being a gracious guest. My employer invites you to join him, and I will take you there."

In the end Nikki went because she was afraid of him.

OUT IN THE HARBOR, at deeper anchorage, there was a yacht that hadn't been there yesterday. Gleaming white, it was bigger than any private vessel Nikki had ever seen. From the mast flew a corporate flag, green with a white triangle, and the letter *M* inside it. Moray pulled the *Reine de Corsica* alongside the yacht. Nikki had some uneasy moments going from the bobbing craft up the ladder of the yacht.

Advancing across the deck was a man who was handsome in a heavy sensual way. He was dressed in dazzling white that set off his high coloring and dark, liquid eyes.

"Miss Damon, you accepted my invitation." Nikki was too speechless to say the things she ought to say. "Welcome aboard. Such a warm afternoon, perhaps you'd like some chilled juice."

Nikki's urge was to refuse with all the contempt she could muster, but the tray of frosted glasses looked so cool, already beading with moisture, and fright had made her throat so very dry.

Nikki drained a glass, and the liquid eased her throat. "I know who you are, Mr. Mohsen," she said. "What do you think you're doing?"

"I am borrowing you, Miss Damon, as I've borrowed other things." He gestured at a chair. "Do sit down."

"Kidnapping is what you mean," Nikki said.

"Miss Damon." His voice was chilling, the world-weary voice of a man whose temper was being tried. "No one has said a word about kidnapping. You are...my guest. When you have served your purpose, you will be returned."

"What exactly is my purpose?"

"Persuasion. I intend to have the lovely opal you've been wearing. You will persuade Mr. Bannerman."

"Is this the kind of persuasion you used to steal Pacific Transport?" Nikki asked.

"I *bought* Pacific Transport, and the owner would have been much better off if he'd sold a year earlier, at my first offer." He looked annoyed. "I told you to sit down."

Nikki's legs were turning to jelly. She sat.

"Better," Mohsen said. "I'm a man of infinite patience, but my little pet has none at all. She wants it now, and I am tired of haggling over price." He called out, "Come here, my dear." A stunning woman appeared on deck, moving with feline grace, a catlike smile upon her face. "Have a seat," said Mohsen. "Mr. Bannerman will be joining us soon."

"I wouldn't count on that," Nikki said.

Mohsen ignored her. "He's probably on his way right now, thanks to your note."

If Mohsen thought a forged note would bring Nile running, he was deluded. Nikki said, "Any note he gets will go straight to the police."

The man remained unruffled. "He won't have the chance, Miss Damon. As soon as you arrived I radioed to have the note delivered. Mr. Bannerman has exactly enough time to make a visit to the hotel safe. My launch will have him here in fifteen minutes."

Brazen plans sometimes worked, but Nikki was certain this one wouldn't.

Unreal! her mind was screaming. Nikki sat at a table covered with fine damask and set with gleaming silver. Her feet rested on a wood deck too beautiful to walk upon. She looked across the water at the postcard-perfect harbor and the hills behind it rising from the sea. Nothing unlovely met her eye, and none of it seemed real.

Mohsen's voice droned on, a smooth and oily sound. "I am a reasonable man." He had a terrifying smile. "I made quite a decent offer."

As his eerily hypnotic stare fixed out upon the water, Nikki's creeping sensation became a conviction. The man was obsessed.

Nikki hadn't seen the small boat coming, but the sound of a motor grew loud enough to break her wary fascination with Mohsen. She left her chair to watch the boat come alongside. Mohsen remained seated like a sultan about to hold court.

Paul Moray went to the ladder as the launch swung clumsily around. "You idiot, come about!" Moray yelled. "You'll hit us!"

Nikki couldn't see the hapless captain, but there was Nile, dark curls windblown, looking more than ever like a pirate about to climb into his nest of thieves.

Nile reached the top of the ladder. Nikki looked behind her at Mohsen, who was still smiling and toying with a wine bottle that was icing in a tall silver stand. Moray walked alongside Nile, who swept one granite-hard, consuming look over Nikki before he turned and went on to Mohsen.

A fanatical gleam lit Mohsen's coal-dark eyes, and Nikki could imagine the blue fire in Nile's.

"Miss Damon," said a voice so unguent-thick it curdled in Nikki's ears, "ask Mr. Bannerman for the opal. Tell him I now can fix his price."

Nile had reached the table.

She couldn't let Nile do it. Mohsen didn't really care about the opal, or even his "little pet." He was only interested in the power to bend people to his whims. Suddenly Nikki plunged her hand into her purse, groping until she found the hard lump she was searching for.

"He doesn't have it!" Nikki cried, yanking the plastic heart free and holding it high above her head. "I do—I've had it all along."

Nikki ran for the ladder but they were coming at her—all of them. She grabbed the rail with one hand and with the other swung as hard as she could, flinging herself almost over the rail in the process. Her feet left the deck.

"No!" The woman's scream was high-pitched, enraged.

"Nikki, no!" Why should Nile try to stop her?

They could all see Mohsen's power over Nile flying from her hand.

Like a fiery comet with a golden tail, the plastic heart flashed red against the sky, the gilt chain flying behind it, then plunged to a watery grave.

"You—" she heard Mohsen scream.

"Nikki, look out!"

Above her in an arc Mohsen's arm was swinging the wine bottle at her. Nikki flung her free hand upward to ward off the blow.

There was a sickening crunch and the sound of breaking glass as he dropped the bottle, but Moray's

weight dropped onto Nikki's hand, breaking her hold
on the rail.

Nikki screamed and fell to the water.

"LIE STILL," someone said. Nikki moaned and tried
to speak. There were hands confining her, and she
struggled. Everything was so black. Disembodied
voices came and went.

A sliver of light sliced the darkness. Someone was
there.

"Nile?"

"Elaine. I'll tell him you asked for him."

Nikki spoke woozily, "Tell him to take..." *Take his
opal and go to*—her unconscious mind worked at finishing the sentence.

"...go to hell."

A strange man gave a friendly snort. "Is that the
thanks I get?"

Nikki's eyes flew open. "Where's Elaine?" she
asked.

The man answered, "There's no one here but me."

Nikki realized that "here" was a hospital room.
"Who are you?"

"Chief inspector, Metropolitan Police." His face
loomed above her. She sat up in the bed, still feeling a
little groggy.

"Where are the police when you need them?" Nikki
asked, not very clearly.

"I drove the launch." He went on to tell her what
had happened, with a policeman's passion for details,
every loose end neatly tied.

"I have so many culprits now, they're outdoing each
other to implicate Mr. Mohsen. And I have him dead

to rights for his assault on you. I'll need your statement, of course."

The chief inspector said nothing about Nile or why he hadn't at least looked in on her. After giving her version of what happened, Nikki asked where Nile was.

"He'll likely be along when I've finished with him." The policeman was in a hurry—he'd gone beyond professional obligations, and now he wanted to leave. At the door he smiled. "You'll be able to wear that opal without fear now, Miss Damon," he said.

"I won't be wearing it at all, Inspector," Nikki said. "I was just bait."

Once fully awake and sure now that Nile wouldn't be coming to see her, Nikki was chafing to leave, but first she had to prove she could stay conscious. Sometime later Sybil came to get her. She was frantic and she wore an expression so shocked that Nikki realized Sybil had gotten no news except that she was in hospital.

Nikki was safe, had no lasting injury, she hurried to tell her friend. She could go home now. But Sybil wanted the harrowing details.

Slowly it sank in that Nikki could have been killed, that Mohsen's overt act, when it came, had been so nearly deadly.

In the taxi Nikki asked, "What about the match?"

Sybil blinked. She'd obviously forgotten the competition completely. "I don't know," she said. "When the hospital called, I just rushed off."

Sybil took Nikki straight to the hotel, and from the glass-walled hall they could hear voices in the playing area.

Someone else was in the hall. "Nikki!" Her name echoed in the corridor, and it caught her unaware, sending her heart leaping. "Thank God you're all right." The sound of Nile's voice sent a flood of longing into every cell. Yet he hadn't even bothered to find out if she was alive or dead.

Nile was struggling in his haste, and he walked haltingly on crutches he hadn't yet synchronized. Nikki flinched, wanting to run, but in which direction?

"Stay here," Sybil said, an authoritative hand gripping Nikki's arm. "I'll get someone to help him."

Nile wasn't quite abreast of Nikki when he barked, "What in heaven's name possessed you to risk your life with a piece of plastic?" He looked furious, and his eyes raked over her with the same penetrating force they had on the yacht.

Nikki wasn't going to answer, and she turned away from the fury in his face. "What's wrong with your leg?" she asked, keeping in step with his uneven progress.

"It hurts like hell, that's what's wrong. Hyperextended," Nile said, shaking his head as if to shake off her questions. "I'll be off these things in a week."

"What happened? Did Mohsen . . . ?" Nikki had a horrible vision of Mohsen's face, twisted with rage.

"It happened when I went over the rail."

Nikki winced. Her own fall into the water from that height had knocked her unconscious. "That monster—he pushed you overboard."

"Nobody pushed me," Nile said. "I did it—well, it wasn't one of my better dives." He sounded exasperated. With himself, with Nikki for evading him and with the crutches he looked ready to throw aside.

It had been lunacy to dive into the water with those boats alongside.

"Why did you do it?" Nikki asked.

"Why?" Nile looked at her as if she were a species from another planet, asking him why he breathed.

"Yes, *why*?" Nikki had been through too much, loved too much, hurt too much, to care any more about her pride. Hurt was stronger than pride, and it erupted uncontrolled. "Why risk your neck for a—a glorified mistress?"

"Mistress? What are you talking about?" Nile's face went ashen gray. "Oh, God, you heard me say— You thought I meant *you*?"

Nikki wasn't listening. Her eyes were squeezed shut, too tight to see what was blazing in his eyes. She made a barricade of her widespread fingers and pushed them against empty air. "I knew it. You warned me." Her hands became fists to pound the air like drums of doom. "You never even hinted anything else."

"Listen to me, Nikki! Stop it! Listen—" His hands imprisoned her wrists, and he drew her near as his words poured in torrents. "If you'd asked me, I'd have told you it was Mohsen's mistress. He gave me an ultimatum, twenty-four hours. I didn't want to tell you... Elaine wanted me to give in, and we argued, but I wouldn't—"

He wasn't going to have the chance to tell her anything more. Sybil was bringing someone from the tournament room.

"Wait!" Nikki cried out, waving them away. She could hardly breathe for fear she'd heard him wrong. "Mohsen's?"

"Yes," Nile hissed into her ear.

"Nile, Nikki, come over here." The tournament director interrupted Nile, stifling the flow of his words but not the urgent message in his eyes.

"Can't this wait?" Nile asked.

"This will only take a minute. We have an unusual situation here."

"I have an unusual situation here," Nile said impatiently. "Can't you settle the rest later?"

The two teams came out from the playing area and gathered around Nikki and Nile. "The match is still tied," the director told them. "We can play into the night, or arrange another set tomorrow."

"Tonight!" No one liked the idea.

Sybil intervened. "They can't play tonight—they're in no condition."

"Tomorrow, then," said the director.

"Just a minute," Nile interjected. "Mrs. Considine?" Nile addressed Sybil formally, and she gave him an equally formal nod. He used the crutches to draw himself erect. "Mrs. Considine, will you accept a tie?"

"This is highly irregular, Mr. Bannerman," the director warned before Sybil had a chance to consider. "Are you asking to withdraw?"

"I am asking to end the match, let it stand as played."

"Give me a satisfactory reason," the director continued to caution, "one that both captains and I agree to. Otherwise, you will forfeit the championship."

"I have a compelling reason," Nile said. "Give me a minute with you and Mrs. Considine, and I'm sure you'll both agree."

The three of them stepped aside for the briefest of conferences and returned to the gathering.

"I accept," Sybil said in a tone that made the walls of the glass hall echo.

"Yes...ah...I also have accepted," said the director. "Under the circumstances, Nikki, I think you should take Nile someplace where he can get off his feet. We'll take care of the results."

NIKKI CLOSED the door, and Nile put his crutches aside. She watched him make halting progress across the room, to stand braced against the bar. There was so much she had to say to him, but it was hard to begin. Instead she asked the least important question on her mind. "How did you convince the director to accept a tie?"

"I reminded him of an old tradition."

"I never heard of a tradition that lets a championship match end that way."

"This one does." Nile looked particularly proud of himself. "Bannermans play together, never against each other. I told him I was going to marry you."

Nikki could barely make herself speak. "Nile, you can't tell people things like that. It isn't true."

There was still a mischievous sparkle in his eyes. "Yes it is—unless you intend to refuse." His expression changed as the seconds passed and Nikki made no reply. "Nikki?"

Her answer came very slowly. "I have to refuse." She turned away from him. "I'd rather you never said that—even in jest—than have you tell me tomorrow it's better to end things than make a mockery of marriage vows."

Nile started to take a step toward her. "But, Nikki, I know you would never take a vow you didn't intend to keep."

Nikki shook her head. "Of course not, and if you didn't intend to keep yours, I—" Her heart almost stopped beating entirely. "It wasn't you..." she whispered. Her eyelids closed over a film of tears. The missing piece of the puzzle fell into place for her. "It wasn't you who didn't plan to keep the marriage vows, was it?"

Nile's eyes were piercing. "No, but I did call off the wedding." He raked a hand through his hair. "I guess I should have done the gentlemanly thing and let Simone—that was her name—end things. But I just flew into a rage when I found out, the day before the wedding, that she'd had other lovers—" his voice became low and menacing "—and planned to continue having affairs after the wedding."

"Oh, Nile... Do you still love her?" Nikki asked, bracing herself for his answer.

"Love her...no. Any love I might have had for her died that day."

Nikki searched his face as if her life depended on it. "Do you even believe in love?"

He answered, "I believe in you."

"Do you love *me*?"

Nile's hands gripped the edge of the bar so hard his knuckles were white.

"Yes."

Nikki took the few steps that brought her into Nile's arms, and he held her tighter and tighter, until finally she heard him say, "I love you, Nikki."

NILE MADE ROOM for Nikki beside him, and she nestled her head into his shoulder. "Ouch!" she said. "There's a lump in your jacket that matches the lump on my head."

Tenderly Nile touched the spot. "You certainly do have a lump on your head." His arm tightened. "You deserve to have one for the stunt you pulled," he said gruffly. He reached into his jacket pocket, saying, "The price for this was to be you, alive. I ought to shake you until your teeth rattle." Nile spoke so fiercely Nikki knew that the emotion behind his words was more than he could bring himself to say.

The velvet box he took from his pocket was ruined from its soaking in sea water. Inside, the opal heart flamed unharmed.

"Nikki, I'm not good with words." He turned the pendant over. "Someone else has said them for me. Read it."

Nikki smiled and did as she was told.

In the depths of his eyes was something wonderful. "That was perfect," he said. "There's hope for your accent yet. Do you know what it means?"

"My heart is in your keeping," Nikki said.

"You translate with such feeling."

Nikki's voice dropped low. "Do you think I'm translating?"

"No, I think you—I know you love me."

SOMETIME LATER Nikki said, "I never dreamed this would happen to me. I feel as if I've won it all."

"I disagree," said Nile. "You wait and see." He hadn't lost the knack of that wicked, wicked smile. "When they finish writing up this match, they'll say, 'The Scores Were Tied, But Bannerman Won The Prize.'"

For once he was wrong. The final headline read, "King of Diamonds Trumped by the Queen of Hearts."

H A R L E Q U I N
Romance

Coming Next Month

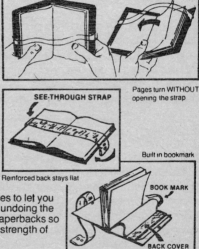

The Pirate
JAYNE ANN KRENTZ

At the heart of every powerful romance story lies a
legend. There are many romantic legends and
countless modern variations on them, but they all
have one thing in common: They are tales of brave,
resourceful women who must gentle and tame the
powerful, passionate men who are their true mates.

The enormous appeal of Jayne Ann Krentz lies in
her ability to create modern-day versions of these
classic romantic myths, and her LADIES AND
LEGENDS trilogy showcases this talent. Believing
that a storyteller who can bring legends to life
deserves special attention, Harlequin has chosen
the first book of the trilogy—THE PIRATE—to
receive our Award of Excellence. Look for it now.

AE-PIR-1A

February brings you ...

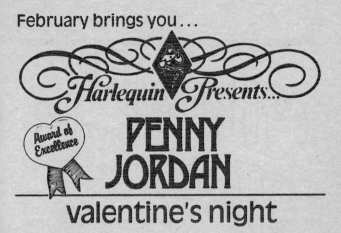

Harlequin Presents...

Award of Excellence

PENNY JORDAN

valentine's night

*Sorrel didn't particularly want to meet her
long-lost cousin Val from Australia. However,
since the girl had come all this way just to
make contact, it seemed a little churlish not to
welcome her.*

*As there was no room at home, it was agreed
that Sorrel and Val would share the Welsh
farmhouse that was being renovated for
Sorrel's brother and his wife. Conditions were
a bit primitive, but that didn't matter.*

*At least, not until Sorrel found herself snowed
in with the long-lost cousin, who turned out to
be a handsome, six-foot male!*

Also, look for the next Harlequin Presents
Award of Excellence title in April:

Elusive as the Unicorn
by Carole Mortimer

HP1243-1

Step into a world of pulsing adventure, gripping emotion and lush sensuality with these evocative love stories penned by today's bestselling authors in the highest romantic tradition. Pursuing their passionate dreams against a backdrop of the past's most colorful and dramatic moments, our vibrant heroines and dashing heroes will make history come alive for you.

Watch for new Harlequin Historicals each month, available wherever Harlequin Books are sold.

History has never been so romantic!

GHIST-1R